DEADLY C

JENNA ST. JAMES

COPYRIGHT © 2021 BY JENNA ST. JAMES.
PUBLISHED BY JENNA ST. JAMES

All Rights Reserved. No part of this publication may be reproduced without the written permission of the author.

This is a work of fiction. Names and characters are either the product of the author's imagination or are used fictitiously, and any resemblance to actual persons, living or dead, business establishments, events, or locales is entirely coincidental.

Deadly Caramel

Chapter 1

"This is amazing." Zoie Stone looked at me and grinned. "I've never seen anything like it. I bet the entire town is here."

I glanced at the massive crowd of supernaturals milling around in the park and nodded. "Pretty much. The July Jubilee is almost a match for our Halloween Festival and our Yule Parade and Christmas Tree Lighting Ceremony."

Zoie frowned. "But why do you call it July Jubilee and not Fourth of July Jubilee?"

I shrugged. "I'm not exactly sure the reason behind it, but the town decided long ago to always celebrate the first Saturday of July. So sometimes it lands on the fourth, sometimes not. But it's still a typical fourth party. The mayor usually grills hot dogs, there are games for kids to play, and lots of contests. My favorite contest is the Wee Little Witches. Witches aged three to five enter and showcase their best spell. There's also a contest for baby werewolves to see who has the best howl. Pretty much every supernatural—leprechaun, vampire, fairy, gargoyle, whatever—has their own talent show of sorts."

"And then we end the night with fireworks," Zoie said excitedly. "That's my favorite part."

I chuckled. "Mine, too, when I was your age."

"Princess! Princess!" Needles, my porcupine bodyguard, zipped over and landed on my shoulder. His wings matched the color of the pink concoction he held in his tiny paws. *"I need more cotton candy. I just can't get*

enough." He crammed the last of the sugary goodness inside his mouth, then licked his paws clean. *"I need more."*

Zoie giggled. "You're gonna make yourself sick, Needles."

"And chubbier," I teased.

Needles gasped and dropped his paws from his mouth, his wings a dark crimson. *"Never! A true bodyguard never loses his svelte figure."*

I was about to tease him further, but my cousin, Serena Spellburn, sidled up next to me. "Tamara and I are ready to take our goodies to the judge's table if you two want to walk with us."

"I wouldn't miss this for the world," I said.

Serena laughed. "It won't be as ferocious as it was when Wendy Wand and Felicity Howler found out we were entering separate mini desserts."

I sighed. "I'm just sorry I missed it. I'd have given anything to witness their reactions."

For the first time in three years, my cousin and her best friend and business partner, Tamara Gardener, were entering separate desserts in the baking contest. They'd won the last three years in a row with Serena's entry of Sea Salted Dark Chocolate Caramel Chew. But Tamara had been working hard to perfect her petit fours, so she entered separately.

Zoie clucked her tongue. "Shame on you, Shayla Loci. Getting pleasure out of other people's misery."

But I could tell from the twinkle in Zoie's eyes she was joking.

Deadly Caramel

"Listen to the sixteen-year-old witch," Needles said. *"She has better manners than you, Princess."*

I stopped walking and cocked my head. "Does anyone else hear an annoying gnat flying around? Someone hand me a fly swatter."

"You better watch your step, Princess," Needles said. *"This annoying gnat can tell your dad stories you'd rather not have repeated."*

"Like what?" Zoie asked. "Stories about my dad and her kissing?"

"What's going on?" Serena demanded. "What am I missing out on?"

It used to be I was the only one who could hear Needles talk, but recently my dad, Black Forest King, granted Zoie a wish for her birthday. She'd wished to hear Needles speak. Why? I have no idea. Now she had that cross to bear too.

"You aren't missing out on anything," I said to Serena. "Needles is just being ornery. Now, let's get your plate of caramels to the judge's table before I decide to sample one."

Serena smacked my hand as I pretended to snatch a caramel. "I left Tamara, Zach, and Baby Jayden by the face painting. Let's go get her and walk over together."

"How's that going?" I asked.

Zoie giggled. "I'd say pretty good considering Zach stops by real quick every day before he goes to work."

"You did good with that matchup," Serena admitted.

I met single-dad Zach, a local bartender, while working on a case last month. He was relatively new to the island and had a one-year-old daughter. In passing, I suggested he visit

Deadly Caramel

the Enchanted Bakery & Brew and meet Tamara. He did...and they'd been dating ever since.

We wound our way through the throng of supernaturals ranging in age from baby stroller to elderly walker. Most were decked out in some version of red, white, and blue clothes.

Baby Jayden smacked her hands together, bounced up and down in her dad's arms, and blew spit bubbles at us when we stopped in front of her. Without warning, she sprang from her dad's arms into mine. I barely had time to react and catch her before she launched into a shrieking and chattering session with Needles.

"She's got healthy lungs." Needles twirled and flipped in the air. The faster he twirled and changed his wing color, the louder Jayden screamed and clapped. *"I think I'm gonna be sick! Too much cotton candy!"*

Laughing, I pivoted and handed Jayden back to her dad. Normally, I'd get a little secret pleasure in seeing Needles lose his lunch, but I knew Serena was eager to get to the judge's table.

"C'mon, silly girl." Zach kissed his daughter's chubby cheek and patted her back. "We'll wait right here for you, Tamara. Good luck to both of you." He gave Tamara a wink. "But I know who I'm rooting for."

"All this love in the air is making my teeth hurt," Needles said.

"That's the cotton candy talking," I joked.

The four of us hurried over to where the judge's table was roped off under a tree. There was already one dessert displayed.

Deadly Caramel

"Why are the desserts all so small?" Zoie asked.

"It's a mini dessert competition," Serena said. "All the desserts have to be bite sized."

"Those look yummy," Zoie said, pointing to a plate of mini moonpies.

Tamara growled low in her throat. "Those are Felicity Howler's moonpies."

"Who's Felicity Howler?" Zoie asked.

Tamara laid her plate down on the other side of the moonpies. "Someone who has made my life a living nightmare for years now."

"Why?" Zoie asked.

Serena snorted. "Too long a story to tell right now. Suffice it to say, there's some bad blood between Tamara and Felicity."

Zoie grinned. "Then I hope her moonpies taste like mudpies."

Deadly Caramel

Chapter 2

"What time will they announce the winner?" I asked as we stepped back from the judge's table.

"Six o'clock," Serena said.

"Excuse me!" a sharp voice said behind me.

I turned and saw Wendy Wand glaring at me.

Mid-fifties, average height and weight, short brown hair cut into a bob to her pointy chin. The witch's green eyes flashed with anger, but instead of focusing on her eyes, I couldn't help but stare at the brown wart nestled against the side of her nose.

"I need to set my lemon bars down." She lifted the plate higher in the air. "The judges need to have access to the grand-prize winner."

"They already do," I deadpanned, motioning to Serena's and Tamara's plates.

"We'll just see about that," Wendy said. "There's no way I can fail this year."

Something in her voice didn't sit right with me. I scanned her plate of mini lemon bars, trying to see if she'd cheated and spelled her dessert somehow, but I didn't see any signs of magic.

"Why is that?" I asked.

Wendy gave me a sly smile. "Let's just say I recently came into contact with a secret ingredient."

I rolled my eyes. "Whatever that means."

"C'mon, Shayla." Serena tugged on my elbow. "I want to go find Grant."

"And Dad will be looking for us," Zoie said.

"Goodie! I haven't tormented the gargoyle in a while," Needles said.

I'd been dating Zoie's dad, Sheriff Alex Stone, for a few weeks now...if you can call it that. Our first date ended up a disaster when we found a dead body. Our next date was better, but with our work schedule, it was almost impossible to really date. Usually what ended up happening was my boyfriend, a gargoyle shifter, would fly himself and Zoie out to my castle and we'd spend the evening having dinner and reading in the library, or I'd help Zoie with her magic. Then he'd fly them back home.

"I guess we should go find the guys," I said.

I let Serena drag me away from Wendy, but to get my bluff in, I kept my eyes on the witch until I could no longer see her...Needles giving her the same death stare as me.

Serena giggled when Needles and I turned back and faced her. "What was that about?"

I shrugged. "I just felt like I needed to be the heavy. Let her know she can't intimidate us."

"She actually *can* intimidate us," Serena said.

"That's no lie." Tamara came to a stop. "I'm parting ways here. I want to take Jayden and Zach to the petting zoo."

Serena, Zoie, Needles, and I headed to where we'd last seen the boys—over by the fireworks display helping to set up. I waved to Mom and Aunt Starla who were handing out water bottles.

"Their favorite job," Serena said.

I nodded. "GiGi must be down at the Wee Witches competition getting ready to judge."

Deadly Caramel

"I want to see that," Zoie gushed. "I bet it's so cute!"

Serena grinned. "Oh, yeah, real cute. Unless you accidentally get on the wrong side of one of their spells."

"I remember that year," Needles said. *"That poor dog never fully recovered from what I understand."*

"What happened?" Zoie demanded.

"Mrs. Mystic's littlest at the time had entered," Serena said. "I think she was four. Anyway, she was supposed to lift the leaf in the air, but she somehow lifted Mr. Moonstone's bulldog six feet in the air before someone finally noticed."

Zoie laughed. "That's so funny. We *definitely* have to go watch the competition now."

Serena motioned Grant and Alex over to where we stood. A couple of the firemen, manning the fireworks station, turned to wave at us.

"What are you girls up to?" Alex said, staring at Needles as he spoke.

"Oh, the gargoyle thinks he's so funny." Needles reached behind him and pulled out one of his quills. *"Let's see how funny he is now?"*

"Hush," I said. "And that goes for both of you."

Grant chuckled. "Did you get your caramel chews turned in, honey?"

"I did," Serena said. "There's going to be a lot of stiff competition this year."

Grant leaned over and kissed Serena lightly on the lips. "You'll do great, Serena. You always do."

"Are you guys going to stay here and finish setting up?" I asked.

Deadly Caramel

Alex nodded. "It shouldn't be much longer. We'll be done before they announce the bake-off winner."

Zoie took a step back from the group. "We're on our way to go watch the Wee Witches competition. I really want to go."

"Have fun," Alex said. "Grant and I will catch up with you in front of the judge's table at six."

Grant gave Serena one more good-luck kiss before the three of us—plus Needles—headed over to the Wee Witches competition. Sure enough, GiGi was one of three judges.

We stood around for at least thirty minutes watching boys and girls ranging in age from three to five show off their best witchy spells. At that age, most baby witches can only lift light objects in the air...which was why the Mystic kid lifting the bulldog earned her first place, even though it was a fluke.

Much to Zoie's disappointment, nothing crazy happened this time around. We were on our way back toward the judge's table when we ran into Mayor Stone and Doc Drago.

"Can't talk long," Doc said. "Mayor and I are in charge of grilling hot dogs again this year. We start handing out at six o'clock sharp."

Mayor Stone grinned. "We look to break a record this year...two thousand hot dogs!"

"You really think you'll give away that many?" I asked.

Mayor Stone shrugged. "They're free. I bet we do."

"So if you girls want one," Doc added, "you better get in line soon. Once they're gone, they're gone."

Deadly Caramel

"Just like I'm sure your desserts will be," Mayor said. "Doc and I took a peek at the table, and for once, I'm glad I'm not judging." He patted Serena's shoulder. "Good luck to both you and Tamara."

We parted company and hurried over to the judge's table. I glanced at my cell phone. "We have about fifteen minutes before the judges start tasting."

"I'm so excited," Zoie said. "I texted Izzy, and she said she'd meet us at the table."

Izzy Fangly was Zoie's best friend. Recently, she'd been kidnapped and held by a killer until Zoie and Needles rescued her.

"I can't wait—" Zoie broke off and stopped walking.

"What's wrong?" I asked.

Shaking her head, Zoie bent over and closed her eyes. "It's nothing. I've been having these weird spells lately."

"What kind of spells?" I demanded, the hair on the back of my neck standing up. "Are you okay?"

Zoie straightened and smiled. "I'm fine. It's just like—I don't know. Like my insides are shifting or something weird like that. It just makes me a little queasy is all."

"Have you told your dad?" I asked.

Zoie shook her head. "I don't want to worry him. Like I said, I'm sure it's nothing."

Needles and I both crossed our arms over our chest—or at least I did...Needles' little arms couldn't reach across his chest. "Zoie Stone, you better tell your father before I'm forced to."

Zoie rolled her eyes like only a teenager could. "Fine. I'll tell him. Can we go now? I'm feeling better."

Deadly Caramel

As we pushed our way through the throng of people gathered around the table, a bubble of excitement fluttered through me. When we finally reached the front, I had to admit, all the desserts looked amazing. I saw Felicity Howler and Wendy Wand standing off to the side.

"I just want to dive head-first into every one of those," Needles said.

"Who has which dessert again?" I asked.

Serena pointed to the end. "Wendy Wand has the little lemon bars, Felicity Howler has the mini moonpies, I have my caramel chews, Tamara has the petit fours, and Carl Feeder has the mini carrot cupcakes."

"Carrot cupcakes?" I mused. "That's an odd entry."

"It's organic," Tamara said as she sidled up next to me. "Carl's entire farm is now an organic farm. He did that about two years ago. His chickens are free-range and organic, all his produce is organic, everything. It's pretty cool out there."

Serena frowned. "Unfortunately, I hear he's having trouble staying afloat now that he's went completely organic. I hate that for him."

"So do I," Tamara said. "I had Zach stand over with Grant and Alex. I'm too nervous for him to be next to me. Is that weird?"

Serena laughed. "Not at all. Hey, I put six caramels on that plate. Two for each of the three judges. Three on bottom, two in middle, then one on top. There's an extra caramel on my plate."

Tamara laughed and took a step toward the table. "Since you hinted to me you and Shayla added an extra

Deadly Caramel

ingredient this year, maybe I'll just steal that extra one and see what I think?"

"Me too!" Zoie said. "I should have a bite."

I laughed. "Too late for Serena to change anything now if it isn't as good as the previous three years."

Serena groaned. "Don't even say that!"

Tamara leaned forward and snatched a dark chocolate caramel off the top of the pile. "Let's see if this is a first-place dessert."

"Maybe you shouldn't," Serena said. "I don't understand how an extra one got there."

But it was too late. While Serena had been talking, Tamara pulled apart the caramel and popped half in her mouth and chewed. She handed the other half to Zoie. "Nice texture, Serena." She put her hand over her mouth and continued to chew. "It doesn't really taste like—"

Tamara stopped talking, lurched forward, and grabbed her throat...her eyes wide and panicked.

"What's wrong?" Serena and I asked simultaneously.

But Tamara didn't answer...instead, she closed her eyes and dropped to the ground.

Deadly Caramel

Chapter 3

Screams and shouts erupted around us, and for half a second, I couldn't think about anything other than Tamara on the ground. I glanced over and saw Zoie's hand—still holding the other half of the caramel—hovering near her open mouth. Without thinking, I smacked the caramel out of her hand. It flew through the air and landed on Felicity Howler's plate of moonpies.

This caused Felicity to scream in rage.

Which was enough to bring me back to reality.

"Someone go get Doc," I yelled. "He's grilling hot dogs with Mayor Stone."

"I think I saw Sean Wolfing by the petting zoo," someone shouted. "He's a paramedic."

"This doesn't look good," Needles said as he dropped onto my shoulder. *"Can I do anything for you, Princess?"*

"I don't know yet." I knelt down next to Tamara, and was about to check her vitals, when Alex and Grant flanked me.

"What happened?" Alex demanded. "We didn't see anything, but heard the shouting."

"I don't know." I laid my ear on Tamara's chest to see if I could hear her heartbeat or hear her breathing. "She picked up an extra caramel off Serena's plate and ate it. Next thing, she's on the ground." I leaned back up and saw a frantic Zach hovering nearby with Baby Jayden in his arms. "I swear I can hear a heartbeat."

"I have a pulse," Grant said.

Deadly Caramel

"Stand back!" Doc shouted. "Everyone, stand back now!"

"My cue," Alex said. "Grant, we need to get control of this crowd."

The two men stood, and I eased back a little to give Doc room to work. I wanted to be close in case he needed me.

"I'm so confused," Serena said. "What happened?"

I ignored her and everyone else shouting around me and focused on Doc checking Tamara's vitals.

"What happened?" Doc asked.

"Tamara snatched an extra caramel off Serena's plate and ate it," I said. "She was talking about the texture of the caramel when she suddenly stopped, grabbed her throat, and collapsed to the ground. Grant says she has a pulse, and I can hear a heartbeat, but she's non-responsive otherwise."

Doc nodded. "Understood. Give me some room here, Shayla."

I scooted back and hit my head on the judge's table. Because I could feel Needles trembling, I reached up and ran my hand soothingly down his back. "Everything is going to be fine."

"My baby!" a voice rang out. "What's happened to Tamara?"

Mom, Aunt Starla, and GiGi hurried over to where Mrs. Gardener was pushing her way through the crowd. When she finally reached us, Mrs. Gardener dropped down next to me. "What's going on?"

Doc shook his head. "I'm not exactly sure. We have a pulse and heartbeat, but she's non-responsive." He opened Tamara's mouth. "Did she choke?"

I shook my head. "I don't think so. If she'd choked, wouldn't she have tried to cough or give us some indication? She just grabbed her throat and fell. She didn't turn blue, nothing."

"It's odd," Doc said as he took a penlight out of his pocket and shined it down Tamara's throat. "There *does* seem to be a sliver of caramel down there." He reached inside Tamara's mouth, and after a few seconds, shook his head and sighed. "I can't seem to dislodge it. How can that be? I can grab hold of it, but it won't budge."

"Magic!" Needles gasped. *"Evil magic."*

"Let me," GiGi said.

"No offense, GiGi," Doc said, "but if I can't get it out, what makes you think you can?"

GiGi and Mom shared a glance.

"Because," GiGi said, "I think maybe a little magic is at play here."

Mrs. Gardener gasped. "Someone put a spell on Tamara?"

GiGi knelt down on the other side of Tamara's body, closed her eyes, and placed her hands over Tamara's mouth. GiGi whispered something under her breath, and a few seconds later she opened her eyes and nodded to Doc. "You should be able to dislodge it now."

"Let's try this again." He reached back in and slowly withdrew the sliver of caramel out of Tamara's throat.

Tamara's eyes snapped open. She sucked in a deep breath, and tried to sit up. "What?"

"Stay down, Tamara," Doc said.

Deadly Caramel

I stood up and let Serena take my place. She thanked me, stroked Tamara's hair, and pushed a calming spell onto Tamara. I could hear Serena whispering words of comfort to Tamara as I scanned the crowd.

"What is it?" Mrs. Gardener demanded. "What happened to her?"

GiGi looked solemnly at Alex. "Sheriff Stone, I think Tamara was given the Sleeping Beauty Spell."

I heard the gasps all around me from other witches.

"That's a banned spell on this island," Needles said angrily, his wings a deep crimson red.

"Are you sure it's the Sleeping Beauty Spell?" I demanded. "I thought that spell fell under the no-no section of things a witch doesn't do on Enchanted Island?"

"It does," GiGi said. "It's also a spell that's hard to find. Very few witches have spell books that old with access to the spell."

"Grant!" Alex called out. "I want every one of those desserts bagged for evidence."

"Yes, sir," Grant said. "I have a field kit in my vehicle."

"How few?" Alex demanded as he herded GiGi and me over by a tree so we couldn't be overheard.

"Excluding myself, Starla, and Serenity? Two other families of witches were tasked with guarding the Sleeping Beauty Spell." GiGi planted her hands on her hips. "You see, Sheriff, folklore around Sleeping Beauty goes back hundreds of years. The French even have a version dating back to the fifteen hundreds. I don't remember the exact year, but at least two hundred years back—because my mom heard about it from her great-grandmother—a witch on Enchanted Island performed the spell on a neighbor she despised. When it was discovered what the witch had done, she was banished from the island and the spell was to be ripped out of every Shadows book a witch had."

"And yet you still have it?" Alex asked. "How come?"

"My ancestors, as well as my late husband's ancestors, were original settlers over three hundred fifty years ago. The coven—there was only one at that time—permitted three books to keep the spell. Those three books were from original settlers whose witches were powerful and knowledgeable. I have access, as do my daughters. And before you ask, yes, they know how to perform the spell."

"You taught your daughters this deadly spell?" Alex mused. "Why?"

GiGi glared at Alex. "A witch of my standing knows many things, Gargoyle. It's not your place to question where I—"

Alex held up his hand. "You're right, GiGi. I apologize."

"Thank you." GiGi shrugged. "That's all I can tell you. The spell can only be found in the three Shadows books. It was a spell lost hundreds of years ago, and I haven't thought about it in decades."

"Let's start with the basics," Alex said. "I assume the Sleeping Beauty Spell is exactly as it sounds? Someone put a spell on the caramel to make the person consuming the candy fall into a deep sleep? How would they wake up? I mean, if it wasn't for you, GiGi, knowing how to counteract the spell, how would the spell be broken otherwise?"

"It wouldn't," GiGi said. "That's why it's a spell that is no longer accepted in any witch coven on Enchanted Island.

There are a couple other spells over the years that have also been banned."

"I called for an ambulance," Sean Wolfing said as he jogged over to stand by us. "Should be here in a few minutes."

"How's Tamara doing?" I asked.

"Surprisingly okay for someone who just underwent a powerful sleeping spell," Sean said.

Deadly Caramel

Chapter 4

"Promise me, Shayla?" Tamara begged. "Please."

For a girl on a gurney who just about died, Tamara's grip was like a vise around my wrist. "I'll do what I can, Tamara. Technically, I'm the game warden now. I can only help investigate if Alex asks me."

"We don't need the gargoyle's permission," Needles said. *"Or at least, I don't. I can handle this little mystery on my own if I have to."*

"Please, Shayla." Tears filled Tamara's eyes. "Find out who did this. Who did this to me."

"We're on it now," Alex said as he sidled up next to me. "Don't worry, Tamara. You just focus on feeling better."

"You'll let Shayla help?" Tamara asked.

Alex grinned and patted Tamara's arm. "Like I could stop her or Needles from helping?"

"Darn right!" Needles cried gleefully, his iridescent wings glowing pale green. *"I'm on the case right now."*

Relief flooded me, but I pretended not to be affected by Alex's words. "It would take an army to stop me, Sheriff Stone." I winked at Tamara. "Isn't that right, Tamara?"

Tamara laughed shakily, then closed her eyes. "Then I'm ready to go to the hospital. Please keep me posted on what you find out."

Alex waved over the two paramedics hovering nearby, eager to take Tamara away. "Grant, Shayla, and I will personally see that you are kept in the loop." Alex brushed his hand over Tamara's cheek. "You focus on getting well."

Deadly Caramel

"Hold up!" Serena called as she jogged over to us. "Tamara, I just spoke with your mom. She, Zach, and I are going to meet you at the hospital."

"What about Baby Jayden?" Tamara asked. "That's not a place for her."

"Zach's aunt and uncle are taking her," Serena said. "The three of us will see you shortly."

Tamara sighed. "I hate I've caused such a ruckus. And on the biggest night of summer celebration we have."

"You let us worry about that," Alex said.

"What about the contest?" Tamara asked. "What'll happen now?"

Alex shook his head. "Sorry. I've had all the desserts taken into the lab."

Taking that as their cue, the two paramedics wheeled Tamara into the back of the ambulance.

"Want to go with me to talk to the contestants?" Alex asked.

I grinned. "I thought you'd never ask."

"I can't believe I'm going to ask this," Alex said, "but Needles, do you think you can stick close to Zoie? I don't want her alone."

Needles laughed and did a somersault in the air. *"I don't think you have to worry about her being alone. Looks like she's got an admirer."*

"An admirer?" I demanded. "Where?"

"What?" Alex demanded. "What's going on?"

Alex and I both whirled around to where we'd left Zoie. Sure enough, Brick Bitely was pressed close to her. In his defense, it looked like he was showing her something on his camera, but I could tell by the way Alex tensed next to me he wasn't happy.

Brick Bitely was built like a linebacker, but had the disposition of a teddy bear. I'd met him a few weeks back when he'd started stalking me. He was an amateur photojournalist and investigative reporter who was entering his senior year in high school. He hoped by following me around he'd stumble across a juicy story that might get him noticed when he applied for colleges on the mainland.

I'd managed to put just enough fear in him that he promised to stop following me...but I also hooked him up with the editor of the *Enchanted Island Chronicle,* Malcolm Luckman. When Izzy's kidnapping story broke, and the killer we were after captured, I gave Brick an exclusive one-on-one to get his foot in the door.

It looked like now he was getting chummy with Zoie. And even though it was probably none of my business, I figured it wouldn't hurt to make sure it was an honest friendship he was seeking, and not something Brick was doing to get information out of Zoie.

"*Never fear, Princess,*" Needles said. "*I'm on it. And if that scallywag tries to put inappropriate moves on Miss Zoie, I'll chop off his hands.*"

"What's he saying?" Alex asked.

"He says not to worry," I said. "He'll make sure Brick is a gentleman."

Needles gave us a salute and zipped over to where Brick and Zoie still stood looking down at his camera.

Grant caught my eyes and jogged over to us. "Tamara is on her way to the hospital. I made sure the three contestants

Deadly Caramel

were quarantined and are now over by the face painting station. I gathered the desserts as evidence and have them marked and ready for Finn to see to on Monday. I can run them by the lab on my way to the hospital tonight."

"That would be great," Alex said.

"What do you want me to do next?" Grant asked.

"I want you to question the three judges," Alex said. "Where were they from—what time did you guys put the caramels on the table?"

"Around five," I said.

Alex nodded. "See where the judges were from five to six. Did they see anything or anyone acting suspicious near the tables? Have they been approached by any of the contestants for a bribe? That sort of thing. You'll know where to go with the questions as you feel them out."

"I will," Grant agreed.

"Also," Alex continued, "talk to GiGi and see who the other two witches are on the island who have access to the Sleeping Beauty Spell. I can't believe I forgot to ask her. We'll want to talk with them shortly. Shayla and I will take the three contestants."

I grinned. "So I take it you aren't questioning Serena? She's not a viable suspect?"

Alex gave me a piercing stare, while Grant chuckled.

"I'll let you know what I find out," Grant said as he turned and walked away.

"Now that it's just the two of us," Alex said, "let me ask you this. Why do you think the would-be killer put the spell on Serena's caramel?"

Deadly Caramel

"Serena has entered the same caramel chew for three years now," I said. "She's won first place with it, so chances are high she'd enter the caramel again this year. Plus, from what I understand, the other contestants all knew what Serena was entering."

"So it wouldn't be too hard for the killer to whip up something that looked like what Serena usually enters. Do you know if all three contestants entered the contest last year?"

I shook my head. "I don't know. I haven't been back for a July Jubilee in many years. I just know Serena wins first place because she tells me."

"Who do you want to question first?" Alex asked.

"Start with the witch," I said. "The most likely suspect."

Deadly Caramel

Chapter 5

Wendy Wand crossed her arms as Alex and I ambled over to where she stood next to Felicity Howler and Carl Feeder. A young girl I didn't recognize stood off to the side next to Carl.

"Wendy Wand?" Alex mused. "Agent Shayla Loci and I would like to speak with you."

"Do I have a choice?" Wendy asked.

"No." Alex shrugged. "I mean, you can refuse, but then I'll detain you and take you down to the station for a formal interview. Or we can just simply step over here and you can answer a few questions for us."

"Fine." She uncrossed her arms and stalked past me. "Let's make it quick."

I stepped in line behind Wendy and followed the two over toward an oak tree. Closing my eyes, I opened myself up to the emotions of the tree and was pleased to find him happy and healthy. I laid my hand on his trunk and gave him a little blessing.

"Ms. Wand," Alex said, "do you have a dessert in the bake-off contest?"

"Yes. My famous lemon bars."

Alex nodded. "And did you enter these lemon bars last year in the bake-off?"

Wendy scowled. "No. Last year I entered my magic bars."

"Do you enter this competition every year?" Alex asked.

"Usually. I think I've entered the last five years."

"And have you ever won?" I asked.

Deadly Caramel

Wendy narrowed her eyes. "No."

"Were you aware," I said, "that Serena was again making her caramel chews?"

Wendy nodded her head once. "I was. So were the other two contestants."

"What time did you drop off your lemon bars?" Alex asked.

"Around five," Wendy said. "Same time as Serena and Tamara."

"You seem a little angry," Alex observed. "Is there a problem here?"

Wendy stared at me. "Not with you, Sheriff."

"With me?" I asked incredulously.

Wendy snorted. "You and your whole family—mom, aunt, grandma, cousin—have always paraded around this island like you're better than the rest of us."

My mouth dropped open. "Excuse me? I hardly even know you, Wendy. I don't think we've ever spoken more than a handful of sentences to each other. I'm not sure where this is coming from?"

Wendy didn't say anything...just continued to glare.

"Anyway," Alex said, "you said you dropped off your lemon bars around five. Where did you go from five until six?"

"I watched the Wee Witches competition for a while."

I frowned. "I don't remember seeing you. Who was your favorite?"

Wendy's eyes met mine, and she gave me a small smile. "I thought little Cassie Cackle showed promise."

That made me pause, because I had to agree with her. Did that mean Wendy was there the whole time? Or did she just know what Cassie Cackle could do?

"I agree," I said. "She has nice control for a wee witch."

"Did you see anyone around the judge's table who shouldn't be there?" Alex asked. "Or maybe something that you thought looked suspicious?"

"Nope. I put my lemon bars on the table and walked away. Everyone is saying someone put an extra caramel on Serena's plate, but I never saw anyone near it."

Alex nodded. "Okay. What time did you go back to the judge's table?"

"Around announcement time," Wendy said. "Like ten till six."

"Okay," Alex said. "Thanks for your help."

"Maybe instead of bothering me, you two should go talk to Felicity Howler."

"Why's that?" Alex asked.

"Because everyone knows Felicity is Hildegard Broomington's housekeeper." She crossed her arms over her chest. "Now, if that's all, I need to get home to my cats."

Alex handed her his business card. "If you remember anything else, please don't hesitate to call."

"And if we have any more questions," I said, "we'll be sure to stop by your place and talk."

In a huff, Wendy turned and marched out of the park.

"So who is Hildegard Broomington?" Alex asked. "Other than another witch?"

"I'm pretty sure we'll find out from Grant or GiGi that Hildegard is one of the witches left on the island who could do this deadly Sleeping Beauty Spell." I shrugged. "Like I said, it's been a while since I was knee deep in Enchanted Island living. But I recognize the last name."

"Then I guess we need to go talk to Felicity," Alex said.

I snorted. "There's a little backstory on Felicity and Tamara."

"Why am I not surprised?" Alex mused. "That reminds me, I need a motive with Wendy. Other than knocking Serena out of the competition, what motive would Wendy have to spell Serena's caramel?"

"I don't know just yet," I said honestly. "I want to talk to Mom about what Wendy said. Maybe she and my family have strife I don't know about. She seems to be angry and holding a grudge. Maybe she thought this was her chance to get Serena out of the picture."

"Could be."

"I know Felicity has more of an ax to grind with Tamara and Serena."

"Let's hear what Felicity has to say."

"Want the background first?" I asked.

Alex smiled. "You know I do."

"Felicity and I are the same age. We graduated together. She's the oldest and comes from a huge werewolf clan family. I think, if I remember right, there are six other younger brothers and sisters. The very youngest, Darren Howler, graduated with Tamara and Serena."

"I sort of see where this is going," Alex said.

"Exactly. In high school, Tamara dated Darren. After graduation, when Tamara and Serena moved to the mainland to attend culinary school, Darren moved too and worked for a construction company. He ended up being a foreman and loved it. After Tamara and Serena graduated and moved back to Enchanted Island, Darren decided to stay. He and Tamara broke up, but amicably. Unfortunately, not everyone in the Howler family was happy Darren stayed on the mainland, and they blamed Tamara."

"And by 'not everyone' you mean Felicity?"

I grinned. "That's about right. Her family owns Howler Landscaping. Last I knew, Felicity worked there, so I'm surprised to hear she's cleaning houses on the side." I shrugged. "She must like the extra money it brings in."

"Why don't I have you go get Felicity and bring her over here?" Alex suggested. "See if she opens up to you without me around."

Chapter 6

"We're ready for you, Felicity," I said. "Hopefully this won't take long."

"I should think not," Felicity said. "I haven't done anything wrong."

I frowned and scanned the area, looking for the young girl who was with Carl Feeder earlier. I didn't see her anywhere.

"So how ya been these last few years?" I asked as we ambled over to where Alex stood under the oak tree. "I haven't spoken to you in ages."

"Don't try and good cop me, Shayla. It won't work."

"Okay. Then we'll just stick to what happened. No pleasantries."

I motioned for her to stand next to Alex.

"Ms. Howler, my name is Sheriff Stone. My partner and I would like to ask you some questions."

Felicity scanned me from head to toe. "I thought Shayla was a game warden. Why is she partnering with you?"

"Sometimes the sheriff's department gets short-staffed, and she's called in."

"Fine," Felicity huffed. "Let me just say right now, I have no idea who poisoned the caramel, and I don't know how to do magic. So obviously I didn't do anything."

Alex held up his hand. "I just want to ask a couple questions. First of all, what time did you put your dessert on the table?"

Felicity shrugged. "Not sure. Maybe a little before five. I was the first person to drop off their entry."

Deadly Caramel

"Where were you between five o'clock and right before Tamara fell to the ground?" Alex asked.

"I mainly just wandered around the park. I went and watched some of the babies howl in the contest being held. I think I grabbed a bottled water from one of the stations."

"You didn't meet up with anyone?" I asked. "Didn't talk to one of your brothers or sisters?"

Felicity narrowed her eyes. "As you well know, one of my brothers doesn't live on the island anymore thanks to Tamara."

"You still have like five others to choose from," I said. "You didn't hang out with any of them?"

"I saw one of my sisters over by the howling contest," Felicity said. "One of her babies had entered the contest."

"You didn't notice anyone suspicious hanging around the judge's table?" Alex asked. "Maybe someone—"

"I already said I didn't," Felicity said.

"You're Hildegard Broomington's housekeeper?" I asked.

Felicity frowned. "Yes. I have been for about five years now."

"But you still work for your family?" I asked.

"Yes. I wanted to bring in a more steady income during the winter months, so I started cleaning houses about five years ago. I only have four I do regularly, but during the slow months, it keeps me afloat. Hildegard is the only house I clean weekly. The other houses are every two weeks."

"Hildegard is quite a powerful witch," I said. "Has she been teaching you magic on the side?"

Felicity scoffed. "No. Why would she? I'm a werewolf, not a witch. I have no magical abilities or use for magic or spells. I'm perfectly content being a werewolf."

"So you're saying she hasn't taught you any magic?" I asked.

Anger flashed in Felicity's eyes. "Why don't you go ask her?"

"We probably will." Alex handed Felicity his business card. "Thank you for your time. If we have any more questions, we'll let you know."

"I'm free to wander around the park?" Felicity asked.

"You are," Alex said.

"Good. I want to get a good seat before the fireworks start."

"Impressions?" Alex asked when Felicity walked away.

"I've not known the Howlers to have magical powers, but that doesn't mean she couldn't have gotten her hands on the spell in Hildegard's house if Hildegard is one of the witches who has access to the spell. As far as motive goes? You heard her say she still blames Tamara for her brother leaving the island." I shrugged. "But here's the thing. I don't see how Tamara could be the target when anyone could have eaten the caramel. It just doesn't make sense."

Alex nodded. "Okay. And Carl Feeder?"

We turned and saw Carl standing alone next to a tree.

"What can you tell me about Mr. Feeder?" Alex asked.

"Not much. Vampire. Mid-forties, I'd say. He has an organic farm outside of town about five minutes north."

"Organic? Really?" Alex mused. "Let's go see what Carl Feeder has to say."

Deadly Caramel

As we walked toward him, Carl Feeder reached back and tightened his thin ponytail to the base of his skull. I had to give it to him...he may be bald on top, but his tail hung down his back. His black skinny jeans paired nicely with his trendy hipster t-shirt, making me smile. The front of his shirt had a picture of *Bunnicula*...a book I'd read as a kid about a bunny rabbit who others thought was a vampire because he liked to suck the juice out of vegetables—especially carrots.

Very appropriate for a guy selling organic vegetables and bringing carrot cupcakes to a bake-off.

"Mr. Feeder?" Alex asked.

"You can call me Carl."

The two men shook hands, then Carl offered me his. His grip was firm, and his shake hardy.

"Carl," Alex said, "can you tell me what time you put your—what did you bring again?"

"Organic carrot cupcakes."

Alex nodded once. "What time did you set your carrot cupcakes on the judge's table?"

"I was the last one. So I'd say around five-fifteen."

"And where," Alex continued, "did you go after you put the carrot cupcakes on the table?"

"My daughter, Darsha, and I split up. She went with her friends, and I walked around the festival."

"Did you go anywhere specific?" I asked.

"Let's see. I believe I watched little ones get their faces painted. Then the vampires had a contest to see which baby vamp had the best set of fangs. That was cute."

Deadly Caramel

"Did you go back to the judge's table at all?" I asked. "After you put your mini carrot cupcakes out, did you ever go back to the table?"

"Nope. Not until it was time to start."

Alex put his hands on his hips. "So you never saw anyone or anything suspicious by the table?"

"No, Sheriff, I didn't."

"Can we talk with Darsha?" I asked.

Carl grimaced. "I'm so sorry. I tried to get her to stick around longer, but she's young and full of energy. She just left with some friends of hers. They are supposed to stay around the park and watch the fireworks later, but I'm not a fool. I can't enforce that."

"How old is Darsha now?" I asked. "I remember Mom telling me when you guys came to live on the island. She thought your daughter was absolutely delightful."

That last part was a bit of a stretch, but I wanted Carl to trust us. It must have worked, because his smile stretched from ear to ear.

"Darsha just turned twenty about two months ago. I couldn't be prouder of her. I've been training her to take over for me one day out at the farm." He held up his hand. "It's a long way off, but one day she'll take over for her old man."

"That's wonderful," I said. "I can see why you're so proud of her and your farm."

"I've worked hard to get Feeder Farm where it is now," he said. "We are the first fully organic farm on the island. It's such an honor for me and Darsha. It took a lot of hard work." He gave me a sheepish smile. "That's why I was hoping so badly to win this year's competition. Having that trophy would just be another feather in the cap, and I was hoping it would bring in more customers."

"In this health-conscious age," I said, "you must do pretty well out at Feeder Farm?"

Carl sighed. "Not as well as I'd hoped. For many, it's still a matter of money. If the food is cheaper, people buy cheaper. It doesn't seem to matter it's full of pesticides and harmful chemicals." He shrugged. "I'm trying to figure out how to educate the masses still."

Deadly Caramel

Chapter 7

"What do you think?" Alex said once we dismissed Carl. "Motive?"

I shrugged. "As far as I know, there's no bad blood between him and any of the contestants or judges. But then again, I'm not up-to-date on everything. I can ask Mom if she's heard anything. I know he said he was hoping to win, but I don't know how giving someone the Sleeping Beauty Spell would help him out."

Alex smiled. "You don't think he'll win with his organic carrot cupcakes?"

I leveled my gaze at him. "Do you?"

Alex chuckled. "Probably not. So maybe it's something we haven't uncovered yet. I'd like to talk to his daughter and see what she has to say."

"I noticed she stood around her dad, just not beside him."

"Meaning?"

I shrugged. "It could be her age, which I totally get, or it could be something more."

Alex scanned the crowd still milling around the park waiting for fireworks. "I'd say our strongest suspects are Wendy Wand and Felicity Howler. Both seem to have personal motives against Serena and Tamara, and both had access to the table. Wendy is the stronger candidate in that she is a witch, while Felicity is a werewolf."

"True," I said. "But we know Felicity is Hildegard Broomington's housekeeper, and Hildegard is a powerful witch. It will be even stronger of a motive if we find out

Hildegard is one of the witches whose family was tasked with keeping the spell safe." I shrugged. "However, I wouldn't discount Wendy too quickly because she's also a witch. Maybe she and Hildegard are friends and Wendy talked Hildegard into helping her. But you're right. I think those two women are our strongest suspects. I'm just not sure if Tamara was the intended victim."

We caught sight of Grant heading our way.

"Hey," Grant said. "I just got done talking with Serena. Tamara is in a hospital room, and they just finished checking her over. There doesn't seem to be any lasting effects from the spell, but the doctor wants to keep her overnight just in case."

I smiled and squeezed his arm. "Good. I can't tell you how scary that was to see Tamara go down so quickly. For half a second, my mind couldn't process."

"I'm just glad you reacted as quickly as you did," Alex said. "Zoie said you smacked her half of the caramel out of her hand."

I laughed. "Yeah, I'm not sure who was more surprised by that."

"I interviewed the three judges," Grant said. "They didn't have much to tell me. None of them were anywhere near the table. The rules state they can't approach the table until the competition. So they were elsewhere in the park during the time of the placement of the extra caramel."

"Dang," Alex said. "Although I pretty much figured."

"I got the name of the two witches who might have access to the Sleeping Beauty Spell," Grant continued. "One witch is Hildegard Broomington, and the other witch is Latrisha Wartski."

"Really?" I demanded. "Well, isn't that interesting?"

"How's that?" Alex asked.

"Wendy Wand is Latrisha's great-niece," I said. "I know Latrisha's family was a founding family, so I guess that makes sense." I frowned. "If I remember right, Latrisha is more a solitary witch. She's had health issues her whole life, so she keeps to herself. But I know for a fact Wendy had a falling out many years ago with GiGi's coven. I wasn't living on the island, but I remember GiGi calling me to tell me about it. When it was all said and done, Wendy was asked to leave the coven." I shrugged. "I think Wendy is part of another coven on the island, but I'm not sure."

"Interesting," Alex said. "Grant, why don't you interview Latrisha, and we'll take Hildegard. Definitely find out if Latrisha may have helped Wendy with the spell."

"Now?" Grant asked.

Alex looked at his watch "No. It's almost eight o'clock. It can wait until tomorrow."

"Good," I said. "Because I'm starving. Let's go see if Mayor Stone has any more hot dogs to hand out."

Grant went to find his grandparents while Alex and I looked for Zoie and Needles and a couple hot dogs to consume.

"Look over there." I pointed to where Zoie, Brick Bitely, and Needles all sat on a blanket surrounded by remnants of food. "Should we go say hi?"

Alex frowned. "What do we know about this boy again?"

Deadly Caramel

Smiling, I grabbed his arm and propelled him through the crowd and dropped down onto the blanket. "What's going on?"

"Hey, Shayla. Hey, Dad." Zoie scooted over to make room for us. "Brick was showing me all the pictures he's taken today."

"And whenever she gets too close," Needles said, *"I send a little cough her way."*

Zoie rolled her eyes at me.

"Can I see those?" Alex asked.

"Yes, sir." Brick handed his digital camera to Alex. "I've probably taken about a hundred pictures today."

Alex didn't say anything, just flipped through the snaps. A few minutes later, he stopped and looked up at me. "Take a look at this."

I leaned over so I could see the camera. "That looks like Wendy Wand by the judge's table."

"Notice the timestamp," Alex said.

"Five-forty," I murmured. "Looks like Wendy was ten minutes earlier to the table than she said."

Alex gave me a small smile. "Something we should ask her about." He handed the camera back to Brick. "Do you think you could look through all these pictures and flag any that show the judge's table? From any angle. Even if the table is in the background. Something might stand out to us."

"Of course," Brick said quickly. "I can do that for you."

"I can help," Zoie said. "Tomorrow is Sunday, and the bakery isn't open. Why don't we meet at the Enchanted Island Café around ten? We can have some breakfast and pour over all the pictures."

Deadly Caramel

Brick cleared his throat then looked over at Alex. "Well, if your dad is okay with it, I'd like that."

We all looked expectantly at Alex...even Needles.

"Fine," Alex said. "You can go. Just be careful you two. Don't let anyone in on what you are doing."

Brick gave Zoie a shy smile, and I reached down and entwined my fingers with Alex's.

"You got anything left over to eat?" I asked.

"Brick brought the basket from home," Zoie said. "There's some chicken and potato salad."

"Perfect." I dug in and handed the food to Alex. "I'm starving."

We'd just finished eating and waiting for the fireworks to start when I caught movement out of the corner of my eye. When I zeroed in on who it was, I gave Alex a little nudge with my elbow.

"Hmm?" Alex murmured. "I'm about asleep here."

"Look."

He followed my finger and sat up quickly. Carl Feeder and Felicity Howler were standing under an elm tree, whispering to each other. A few seconds later, Felicity looked around and leaned back in to whisper something in Carl's ear. He nodded, and the two of them parted ways.

"That was odd," I said.

"Maybe Carl isn't as innocent as we first thought," Alex said.

I patted his hand. "How about I pick you up in my Bronco around nine tomorrow morning? It's a Sunday, so no sense getting Hildegard up too early."

Alex narrowed his eyes. "You just want to drive."

Deadly Caramel

I grinned. "You're right."

Alex laughed and pulled me closer to him.

"Gross," Zoie said behind us. "Brick, Needles, and I don't want to watch you two get all adult mushy."

"The gargoyle better watch where his hands go," Needles said. *"I might just have to lop them off if he gets too handsy."*

Zoie giggled.

"Do I want to know?" Alex asked dryly.

"Nope," I said.

"Hey!" Zoie pointed to the sky. "Look up there. Is that Doc?"

Sure enough, Doc Drago and a couple of his dragon and wyvern friends flew through the night sky. A few seconds later, the darkness exploded with light and the fireworks show was under way.

Deadly Caramel

Chapter 8

I made a pit stop before heading home after the fireworks show. Serena texted me and said Tamara was in her own room at the hospital and getting ready to call it a night. I figured I'd stop by real quick and see how she was doing.

Needles was curled up next to an enormous bag of cotton candy, snoring loudly. I left him in the Bronco, rolled down the windows, and jogged to the hospital entrance.

"Good evening," the woman behind the desk said. "How can I help you?"

"I'm here to see Tamara Gardener. She was brought in earlier."

"Oh, yes." The woman clucked her tongue. "Terrible thing that happened." The woman bit her lip. "Technically, visiting hours are over, but..."

"It's okay." I pulled out my badge. It said game warden, but most people didn't look too closely. "I'm helping Sheriff Stone and Detective Wolfe with the investigation."

"Oh, then go right ahead. She's on the second floor, room two-fifteen. Have a good evening."

I thanked her and hurried to the elevators down the hallway. The doors slid open, I punched the number two button, and waited impatiently for the doors to close.

The second floor was dimly lit when I stepped out of the elevators. I followed the numbers on the wall until I reached Tamara's room. I heard voices inside and pushed open the door.

"Can I join this party?" I joked.

Deadly Caramel

"Shayla!" Tamara and Serena both said.

"Mom just left," Tamara said. "Zach left about half an hour ago. I'm about to get some rest."

"I won't keep you long," I said. "I just wanted to stop by and see how you're feeling."

Tamara shook her head. "I can't believe this happened. Do you know who put the extra caramel on Serena's plate yet?"

"Not yet. Alex and I are questioning more people tomorrow."

Serena twirled the engagement ring on her finger. "Grant said none of the judges saw anything. I told him to tell Alex since the bakery is closed tomorrow, if he needs me as a backup deputy, I'm willing to help out however I can." She reached over and held Tamara's hand. "I want to find out who did this."

"We all do," I said. "Let me ask you guys, do you think Tamara was the intended target, or one of the judges?"

Serena shrugged. "I don't know any of the contestants who would want to do physical harm to one of us. I mean, I know Felicity holds a grudge against Tamara, but I can't see her doing something like this."

"Me, either." I sighed. "I'm thinking maybe one of the judges may have been the intended target, but I have no motive yet."

"You'll figure it out," Tamara said. "You always do."

"I better head out," I said. "I still need to tell Dad what happened. It'll be a late night for me."

"Thank you for helping me, Shayla," Tamara said. "I know there's not exactly been a murder or anything, but I appreciate how you and everyone else is treating it seriously."

"It was a deadly spell that's been banned," I said. "Of course we'd treat it seriously." I leaned down and kissed Tamara's cheek. "Sleep well and blessed be."

Serena walked me out into the hallway.

"Thanks for stopping by." She gave me a hug. "I'm going to head home soon too. I just hate to leave her while she's still awake."

"Think about the contestants and the judges," I said. "Let me know if you can think of any motive one of the bakers would have to harm a judge."

"Will do."

***

"What a night, Needles." I tied my running shoes and did a couple stretches. "Not that I want to stay out late, but I think I need to let Dad know what happened, and that the banned spell was cast."

"I agree."

We took off around the back of the castle and down the trampled lane. I was in my own world thinking about motives and suspects when a giant ball of light headed my way. The closer it got, the louder the squeals and chatter got.

"Princess! Did you see the fireworks?"

"How was the festival?"

"Did you bring us a treat?"

"Did Serena win the contest?"

"Black Forest King enjoyed the fireworks."

Deadly Caramel

"So many questions," I panted.

"I brought cotton candy." Needles held out his two front paws, thrusting the pink sugary goodness at the lightning bugs. *"Have some and be gone!"*

More squeals as they all raced toward Needles. I tried not to laugh as the cotton candy got smaller and smaller in his paws. His wings shimmered from green to yellow in his pleasure. He wouldn't say it out loud, of course, but I knew Needles enjoyed the attention.

"Now that your bellies are full, get on out of here." Needles stuffed the last of the cotton candy in his mouth. *"Nothing left here for you."*

I laughed. Pink sugar crystals still clung to Needles' wet mouth. "You're gonna be so sick, Needles."

"Better me than them," he said with a grin.

I slowed down at the entrance of Black Forest in front of my favorite pine tree. "Good evening, Mr. Pine. I'd like to see Dad."

"Black Forest will be thrilled to see you, Shayla." The pine lifted his large branch off the forest floor, and I dashed inside.

Standing up, I closed my eyes and inhaled deeply. The first initial impact of Black Forest was almost indescribable. It was pure euphoria—peaceful and serene. If the calming effect the forest had on people could be bottled and sold, billions would be made.

My dad was a genius loci, which meant he was literally the heart and essence of Black Forest. Everywhere I looked, I could feel his presence.

His lifeblood.

Deadly Caramel

"*Thank goodness we made it inside before I lost my guts.*" Needles did a somersault in the air. "*Why did you let me eat so much cotton candy, Princess?*"

I laughed and hurried after Needles, anxious to talk to Dad. We ran for a few more minutes through the forest until we reached the clearing where Dad lived.

My dad...the tree.

His tree roots were at least four feet tall and extended out of the ground about twenty feet from the base. His trunk was over one hundred twenty feet around, and his branches—which averaged about thirty to forty feet—were strong and thick.

"*Shayla! Daughter of my Heart.*" Dad's soothing, deep voice filled my head. "*It is so good to see you.*"

I jumped up on one of his massive roots and ran down the length of him, plopping down at the base of his trunk. "Hey, Dad. The fireflies tell me you all watched the fireworks."

"*Indeed. Once again a most spectacular show.*"

"You may need to keep an eye on the lightning bugs," I said. "Needles stuffed them full of cotton candy."

Dad's booming laugh filled my head. "*It's been many years since Needles attended the July Jubilee in town. I assume he not only stuffed the fireflies, but he stuffed himself as well?*"

"*Guilty, Black Forest King.*" Needles dropped down onto my shoulder and leaned into my neck. "*I am not as young as I once was. I may have overindulged a wee bit.*"

Deadly Caramel

"*An overindulgence every now and then is just what is needed,*" Dad said. "*I'm glad you all had an enchanted evening.*"

"Not all of it was wonderful," I said. "We did have a minor snag."

"*What happened, Shayla?*" Dad asked.

I quickly filled him in on Tamara and the Sleeping Beauty Spell she ingested. Before I finished my story, Needles' soft snores brushed my ear.

"GiGi told Alex about how the spell was banned, and how only a handful of witches on the island have access to the spell—GiGi being one. Tomorrow, Grant is questioning Latrisha Wartski, and Alex and I are questioning Hildegard Broomington."

"*I know Hildegard well,*" Dad said. "*She was the wise witch I used nearly forty-one years ago to help me build the castle you live in now.*"

"Really? I didn't know that."

"*Few did,*" Dad said. "*I wanted it kept a secret. I didn't want to cause bad feelings between GiGi and any of the witches in her coven.*"

"Makes sense," I said.

"*Please keep me informed on what you find out. And I'm sorry to hear about Tamara. I hope she recovers fully and is able to go home tomorrow.*"

"Me too, Dad." I leaned back against his trunk and sighed. "One night, I'm going to have to camp out right here."

47

Deadly Caramel

Dad chuckled. *"It is a sight I never grow old of."* He was quiet for a moment. *"Because I love you, I will caution you to be careful, Shayla."*

"I will, Dad." I stood and wrapped my arms around his trunk the best I could. "Now, I better wake up Needles and get back home. I love you."

"And I love you, Daughter of my Heart."

Deadly Caramel

Chapter 9

"I think I visited out here once when I was a little girl," I said as I drove down Hildegard's driveway the next morning. "GiGi would take me with her to her coven meetings on special occasions. If I remember right, they had a party out here once after—well, probably a summer solstice or winter solstice meeting."

"Is Hildegard around Gigi's age then?"

"Yes. Hildegard is probably pushing eighty by now."

I made the small left bend in the forested driveway, then drove another thirty feet before I came to a clearing among the trees. The large home would have done any scary movie justice. It was three stories tall, dark gray, with black shutters. It reminded me of the house in the movie *Psycho*.

Alex shot me a grin. "Did you have nightmares after visiting here when you were young?"

"You know it."

Alex laughed. "I can imagine."

"Tell the massive gargoyle it's too early in the morning for him to flap his tongue," Needles grumbled from the backseat.

I looked over my right shoulder. "No one said you had to come today."

Needles shot me a glare before turning to pout at the door. He was too tiny to see out the window when he was sitting in a seat.

"What's his problem?" Alex asked.

"He has a sugar hangover. Too much cotton candy."

Alex laughed. "That's a hangover I've never heard of before." He leaned forward to peer out the windshield. "What in the—are those crows lined up on the roof of Hildegard's house?"

I leaned over the steering wheel and squinted up at the roof. Sure enough, six black crows were perched on the edge of Hildegard's roof. As I came to a rolling stop, I swear I could feel their beady, black eyes watching our every move. "You know what they call a group of crows clustered together, right?"

Alex unbuckled his seatbelt and opened his door. "A murder." He shut the door and looked up at the rooftop again.

I opened my door and hopped out. "That doesn't bode well."

"It sure doesn't," Alex muttered.

Needles zipped out my door before I closed it. *"Don't worry about tuning into their emotions. I think I'll fly up there and see what the crows have to say."*

"Good idea," I said.

Needles took off toward the rooftop.

Alex watched Needles for a few minutes—his wings fluttering fast as he hovered in the air to talk with the crows—then fell into step beside me.

"I'll go ahead and take the lead if that's okay?" I jogged up the front steps. "Since she knows GiGi, I figure that will be to our advantage."

"That may not be necessary." Alex pointed to the door, which was slightly ajar. As one, we both whipped out our guns from our holsters. "Hildegard Broomington? Are you in here? This is Sheriff Stone. I'm coming in. I have Agent Shayla Loci with me."

As he pushed the door open, I checked over my shoulder to make sure everything was clear, then followed him inside. The foyer and wooden staircase split the house into two separate sections.

Broken glass from a shattered vase lay against the floorboard of one wall, an overturned antique table sat in the middle of the foyer, and three other wooden pieces of furniture lay smashed around the room. Signs of a struggle...just not a typical struggle. More like the items had been flying through the air when they'd been destroyed.

"Hildegard Broomington?" Alex called out again.

When there was no answer, Alex's eyes met mine, and with his hands he motioned that he would clear left, and I would clear right.

With the nod, I went through the archway to my right. The dining room was in an "L" shape that led into the kitchen. There were a couple dirty dishes in the sink, a kettle on the stove, and a bowl of fruit on the table. Otherwise, the kitchen was spotless.

I headed back to the foyer.

"No one in the parlor or library," Alex whispered. "Let's clear the second floor."

Once again, with our weapons drawn, I followed Alex up the stairs. There was a wall to my right, so I positioned myself so my back was toward the wall as I slowly crept up the stairs, covering both Alex and myself.

At the top of the stairs, Alex motioned for both of us to clear the room on the right. Since the door was open, all we had to do was cross the threshold. Alex cleared the en suite bathroom, while I checked the closet and under the bed. I had to give Hildegard props for being able to still walk up and down the stairs at her age. Once the room was searched, we stepped back out into the hallway.

"Let's clear the rest of the rooms on this floor," Alex said. "Then hit the third floor."

We headed down the hallway, bypassing the next set of stairs that led up to the third floor, and instead cleared each of the two rooms and one bathroom on the second floor. Still no sign of Hildegard.

"I say we see what's on the third floor," I said.

"Princess! Princess! Are you up here?" Needles zipped down the hallway toward us, his wings dark purple and fluttering fast. *"Princess, the crows say they haven't been fed for at least three suns—which I took to mean three days. According to them, the Hildegard witch feeds them daily."*

"The crows say they haven't been fed in a couple days," I said as Needles dropped onto my shoulder.

With a small nod, Alex headed up the stairs to the third floor, me following on his heels. We hadn't even reached the top of the stairs, when I sucked in my breath.

"I know that smell," I gasped.

Alex glanced back at me and nodded. "Yeah. I can see an open door with feet sticking out of the doorway."

We both rushed down the hallway to where the body lay face down on the floor, half in and half out of the room.

"It's Hildegard," I said. "GiGi gave me a description."

"I don't have a pulse," Alex said. "Not that I expected one. Doc will need to confirm, but I'd say she's been dead at least a couple days."

I stood and looked around. "What did the killer do? Make Hildegard open this door, and then hit her over the back of the head so she fell straight down?"

"Black Forest King will not be happy," Needles said. *"He always respected Hildegard."*

"Needles is right," I said to Alex. "My dad is not going to be happy. He was a fan of Hildegard."

Alex stood. "Is this the room where she practiced?"

"I think I'll just wait out here, Princess," Needles said. *"Protect the hallway and make sure the killer isn't still around."*

"You don't have to come inside, Needles." I knew the fierce protector had a sensitive side and didn't like being around dead bodies.

I stood in the center of the room and ran my eyes over the books, the small altar in the middle of the room, and the myriad candles set about. "Oh, yeah. I'd say this is where Hildegard practiced." I walked over to where an empty podium sat. "There was something sitting right here. You can tell because there's a slight outline of dust particles that only hit the outer edge. The center is smooth and dust free."

Alex ambled over to where I stood. "Let me guess. This is where she kept her generational Book of Shadows? The one that probably held the Sleeping Beauty Spell?"

"More than likely."

"I better call this in," Alex said. "Doc needs to get the body, and since Grant is talking to Latrisha this morning,

Deadly Caramel

and Deputy Sparks is on patrol for the island, that leaves you and me to secure the scene and gather the evidence."

Needles hovered in the doorframe above Hildegard's body. *"How is it you always manage to drag me into these situations, Princess?"*

"Just lucky, I guess," I quipped.

Chapter 10

"I got dried mud or something over here," I called out from the hallway.

Alex stepped over Hildegard's body and squatted down next to me. "Mud? Not blood?"

"Luminol test is clear. It's not blood." I motioned to the field kit I'd gotten out of my Bronco after we called Doc. Needles volunteered to wait outside until Doc and the paramedics arrived to show them inside. Even though the ambulance wouldn't be necessary, Doc still needed the paramedics' help to get Hildegard on the stretcher and into his vehicle.

Alex frowned. "Must have been on the killer's shoes."

"Could be," I agreed. "I'll bag it and give it to Finn just in case."

Alex stood and stretched. "Let's talk about what we assume is the missing Shadows book. Thinking about our suspects, who is going to benefit more from stealing it? Another witch? A werewolf? Or a vampire?"

Sealing the evidence bag, I placed it inside the field kit for safekeeping, then walked over to where Alex stood. "That's the thing. I want to say another witch for sure, but I guess if said werewolf or vampire have magical abilities, it would work for them."

"I thought only advanced or powerful witches could do the spell?" Alex mused.

"Only three witches had *access* to the spell because it's been banned," I corrected. "I guess technically any witch or any supernatural with the ability to wield a little magic could perform the spell if they had it."

"We know Wendy is a witch, and we're pretty sure her great-aunt has access to the spell. This thrusts her high on my list."

"Then why steal Hildegard's Book of Shadows?" I asked. "If Wendy has access to her great-aunt's book, why go to this much trouble?"

"Good question," Alex said. "I can't believe I didn't think of that. But you're right. Unless her great-aunt, Latrisha, refused to help Wendy, then maybe Wendy needed to kill Hildegard for it."

"Could be." I shook my head. "I don't know why, but I'm still circling back to Felicity Howler."

"Which makes the most sense," Alex said. "We know she cleaned Hildegard's house, which means she would have access to this room, or at least knew what was hidden behind the door of this room. Plus, we know she's not a fan of Tamara or Serena."

"As far as I know, Felicity can't do any kind of magic on her own, but she has plenty of friends who are witches. She's pretty much lived on the island her entire life. If she got her hands on the Sleeping Beauty Spell, I'm sure one of her friends would help her perform it. Mainly because it's as elusive as the Holy Grail."

"Do you know if Carl Feeder has any magical abilities?"

I shook my head. "As far as Carl goes, he and his daughter moved to the island like five years after I left to join the Paranormal Police Department. I just remember Mom telling me about them. I have no idea what his family history is outside of vampire."

"Something to check on," Alex said.

"Sheriff? Shayla?" Doc's voice rang up the stairs. "Are you two up there?"

Alex walked to the stairs and leaned over the railing. "We are. We're on the third floor."

A few minutes later, Doc strolled down the hallway, medical bag in hand, his polished wingtips gliding softly over the floor. Behind him, two paramedics followed, carrying a stretcher.

"I can't believe someone murdered Hildegard Broomington," Doc said as he stared down at the body. "She was such a nice old witch."

"Mainly need time of death," Alex said.

Doc nodded. "Like usual, I can give you an approximation. I'll know more once she's on the table."

"Understood," Alex said.

Doc squatted down next to the body for a few minutes. "I'd say she took a blow to the temple and right side of the skull." Doc glanced at his watch. "By the time I get her back to my lab and get started, it'll be around noon. Hopefully, I should have preliminary findings for you by three."

"That would be great," Alex said. "I'll need to know her next-of-kin, if she had any."

I pursed my lips in thought. "Didn't she have a son?"

"She does," Doc said. "Isaac. He and his wife live about ten miles from here. The problem is, they're on vacation this week. They're doing a supernatural cruise through the Bermuda Triangle. They are totally out of reach. But I'm sure you can go through the Supernatural Coast Guard and they can patch you in to the ship, Sheriff." He looked back down at Hildegard, sorrow etched on his face. "About once a month a group of us all go out to eat, that's how I know about the vacation."

I sighed. "I hate this part of the job."

"I can call the Supernatural Coast Guard," Alex said. "Not how I'd want to give out this kind of information, but it's all I can do."

"I'd stay here and be present when you inform Isaac," Doc said, "but I need to get started on Hildegard as soon as I can. It's what I can do for Isaac and his wife."

I gave him a quick hug. "I'll be sure and give your condolences."

"Thank you. Now, give me a minute, and I'll have an approximate time of death for you in case you need to get alibis later today."

My cell vibrated, and a text from Serena came through. "Looks like Tamara was just released from the hospital."

"Good to hear," Doc said. "I have approximate death around Wednesday night, say nine pm until nine the next morning. Also, I have a lot of bruising on the back of the calves, like maybe she was dragged up here to the third floor. Like I said, I'll know more when I get her on the table." He stood, picked his medical bag off the floor, and motioned the paramedics forward. "I'll call you around three with everything else."

Deadly Caramel

Chapter 11

By the time Alex made the dreaded call to Isaac Broomington, and we locked up, it was a little after ten-thirty.

"Before we go out to the Feeder Farm," Alex said, "I'd like to stop by Enchanted Island Café and check on Zoie and Brick."

"You got it."

Fifteen minutes later, I parked along the curb in front of the café, and Alex, Needles, and I headed inside. The two teenagers were seated in a booth at the back of the restaurant, heads bent together.

"I'll put a stop to this." Needles plucked a quill off his back and zoomed over to their table. *"Two feet apart at all times, you hormonal teenagers!"*

Zoie jerked back and scowled at Needles. "What are you doing here?"

"Protecting your honor," I joked as Alex and I folded ourselves down into the booth.

Zoie rolled her eyes. "Seriously. All three of you?"

"We're actually here for a specific reason," Alex said. "But first, have you found anything?"

Brick handed Alex a stack of photos. "These are all the photos we've come across where the judge's table can be seen. I stayed up most of the night going over the digital photos so I could print them off this morning. We're just rechecking everything on the digital camera to make sure I didn't miss anything."

"That's a little over-achieving," I said.

Brick grinned. "I didn't want to let you guys down on my first big assignment."

"*Suck up*," Needles scoffed as he sat down on my shoulder and nibbled on a broken-off piece of biscuit.

Alex flipped through the first couple pictures. "Anything stand out to you?"

Brick shook his head, his face crestfallen. "Not really, sir."

"Howdy, newcomers." Flo Roundtree—a perky, middle-aged fairy with a beehive hairdo, pencil behind her ear, and electric blue eyeshadow—blew a bubble and snapped it back inside her mouth. "What can I get for ya?"

"I'm fine," I said. "We can't stay long, Flo. Just wanted to touch base with Zoie and Brick."

Flo nodded. "These two youngsters have been sitting in this booth for over an hour now pouring over some pictures." She slapped her pad against her hand. "Well, if you need anything, just holler."

I waited until she walked away before turning to Brick. "You're sure? Nothing stood out?"

"These three may hold some promise." Zoie slid the photos to me. "I think so, anyway."

"This is the one that shows Wendy at the table with the timestamp of five-forty," I said. "This one looks like someone reaching across the table. Does anyone recognize this person?"

Alex took the photo from me, but then shook his head. "I don't know who it is, but you're right. It does look suspicious."

Deadly Caramel

"This last one," I said, sliding the picture to Alex, "if I didn't know better, I'd say that's Darsha Feeder near the table. Timestamped around five-thirty."

"Darsha?" Alex mused. "What was she doing there?"

I smiled. "Guess we'll ask her when we question her next."

"Nice job, Brick." Alex handed the photos to his daughter. "I appreciate both of you helping out."

"Did you need us to do anything else?" Brick asked eagerly.

Alex frowned. "Sort of. I'm afraid I have some bad news. Shayla and I went to interview Hildegard Broomington this morning, and we found her dead in her house. She'd been murdered."

Both teens gasped.

"That's awful," Zoie gushed. "Who would do that?"

"That's what we're working on," Alex said. "I actually want Needles to stay with you today, Zoie. I don't like the thought of you being alone with a killer running around on the island."

Brick cleared his throat and sat up straighter. "I can hang with Zoie today too." He held up a hand. "I mean, if that's cool with you, Sheriff Stone."

Alex smiled. "You can call me Alex." He looked at Zoie. "Is that okay with you?"

Zoie fluttered her lashes at Brick. "Yeah, that's okay with me."

"*And it's okay with me too.*" Needles twirled his quill and rocked his head from side to side, as though cracking his neck. "*I haven't had a good rumble since the last time I took* on the gargoyle. I'm ready to take on a vicious killer or a handsy boyfriend. Doesn't matter to me."

"Daaad," Zoie whined. "I don't need Needles hanging around."

"Of course you do," Needles argued, his wings shimmering purplish red. *"No one will lay a hand on you as long as I am near."*

Zoie sent me a "help" look, but before I could run interference, Alex sighed. "I know it will probably be a nuisance, but could you please just humor me and let Needles stay with you?"

Zoie smiled. "Of course. I know you have a lot on your mind."

Alex leaned over and kissed Zoie's cheek. "Thanks. Now, we need to go see a couple suspects today." He placed some bills on the table. "Breakfast is my treat. Especially since you gave us a clue, Brick."

Brick beamed. "My pleasure. Anytime."

Deadly Caramel

Chapter 12

Feeder Farm was located about five miles north of town off Enchanted Way Road. As I drove over the cattle guard, I couldn't help but be impressed with what Carl had done with the plot of acreage he had.

The main house sat just ten yards off the road, but the driveway continued past the house and straight to a red barn with a Feeder-Farm-Organic sign across the front. Next to the barn was a fruit and veggie stand. To the right of that was a massive fenced-in area of about three acres where roosters and hens ran amuck.

Carl Feeder, dressed in red skinny pants and a t-shirt with Foghorn Leghorn on the front, strolled out of the barn as I pulled to a stop in front of the stand. Darsha was arranging fruits and vegetables in baskets and barely glanced our way.

"Hello," Carl called. "What can I do for you today?"

"Shayla and I need to speak with Darsha about yesterday," Alex said. "And then we'd like to ask you a few more questions, Mr. Feeder."

"Of course." He took off his hat and wiped his brow with a handkerchief. "You hear that, Darsha? The Sheriff and his partner need to talk to you about the horrible incident that happened yesterday."

Darsha smiled and rolled her eyes. "Of course I heard, Dad. I'm standing right here."

He grinned at her. "Just making sure."

Laughing, Darsha motioned us over to where she stood next to a basket of plump, ripe blueberries. "Good morning.

Deadly Caramel

Pay no attention to my dad. He thinks he's a comedian most days." She motioned to the basket. "Care for a handful while we talk?" She tossed two in her mouth. "Best part of the job."

I plucked one off the top and popped it in my mouth. The intense flavor was surprising, and I couldn't stop the moan. "Amazing."

"Right? Since we've gone all organic, our produce has never tasted better." She shoved her hands in her front pockets and smiled. "I'm a little nervous. Dad said you'd probably need to talk to me. I don't think I know anything, but I'll try and help."

Alex nodded. "That's all we ask. Did you go with your dad to put his organic carrot cupcakes on the judge's table?"

"No. I stood off to the side and waited for him."

"What time was that?" Alex asked. "Do you remember?"

Darsha bit her lip and scrunched her nose. "Maybe around five-fifteen or so."

I reached down and picked up another blueberry. "Did you see any of the other contestants near the dessert table?"

"No. Just Dad."

"After your dad put his entry on the table," Alex said, "what did you guys do next?"

Darsha shrugged. "Well, we went separate ways."

"What did you do?" I asked.

"Hung out with friends." She glanced away as Carl ambled over to stand by us. "Just ran around mostly."

"Are you sure?" Alex mused. "Because I have a timestamped photograph that shows you at the judge's table around five-thirty. Can you tell me what you were doing?"

Deadly Caramel

"Darsha?" Carl asked. "What's the sheriff talking about?"

Darsha sighed. "I wanted it to be a surprise, Dad." She took her hands out of her pockets and crossed them over her chest. "Unfortunately, once Tamara got sick, they confiscated the desserts so you didn't get a chance to see."

"See what?" Carl asked.

"You know how I said the tops of the carrot cupcakes needed something to make them pop?" Darsha asked.

Carl scowled. "Yes. And I said no way are we putting a carrot made of pure sugar on top. It's an organic cupcake."

Darsha threw up her hands. "See, Dad. Right there. That right there is why I can't talk to you! I didn't mean you needed to slap on one of those gross hard sugar decorations. I wanted to do something that looked like what the fancy restaurants do with sugar, only not with sugar."

"What do you mean?" I asked.

"Instead of spinning sugar, like those hard webs they put on top of fancy desserts," Darsha said, "I found a way to spin organic honey. Gives it a crystalized look. It worked great, and it wasn't sugar. So I made up a bunch, and when Dad wasn't looking, I went to the judge's table and put them on top of the cupcakes."

"Why would you do that?" Carl demanded. "It wasn't your place, Darsha. I want people to see the natural product, not some sugary substance."

Darsha groaned. "It wasn't sugar, Dad! It's organic honey. And that's your problem. You can't see the big picture. Your entry wasn't going to win because it lacked—"

Deadly Caramel

"If you didn't like the Feeder Farms Organic Carrot Cupcake entry," Carl said smoothly, "then you could have entered your own dessert, Darsha."

"Why do you have to be so bullheaded about everything?" Darsha demanded. "I'm only trying to help get this place recognized!"

Carl shook his head, and I had to look away from him because he suddenly looked ten years older. I hated getting in the middle of Dad-Daughter fights. Mainly because I could empathize with both sides.

"Darsha, I know you love this place and only want what's best," Carl said, "but you need to remember that I am still in charge. You're still so young and have a lot to learn. I have ideas I'm working on. I've even been thinking about bringing someone in to help—"

He stopped talking when Darsha burst into tears and ran crying from the tent, down the path, and up the back stairs into her house.

"I'm so sorry you had to see that," Carl said. "I love my daughter, and I know she loves this place, but I have certain principles that I won't compromise. And I don't blame her for adding the extra decoration on top of my dessert. She's only doing what she thinks she needs to do." He sighed and stared down at his house. "Is she in trouble for messing with the judge's table?" He gasped. "I mean, she didn't admit to putting the spelled caramel that hurt Tamara on the plate, she just admitted to tampering with my dessert. Trying to make it more aesthetically pleasing to the judges."

"She's not in trouble," Alex said. "We bagged all the desserts and will have our forensic technician test the topping she talked about. If it is simply an organic honey topping, then I have to assume Darsha is telling the truth as to what she was doing at the judge's table around five-thirty."

"Thank you," Carl said. "I don't want her getting in trouble for trying to help me out."

"I do have a couple follow-up questions for you, Mr. Feeder," Alex said. "It shouldn't take long."

Surprise flickered across Carl's face. "Oh, sure, Sheriff. How can I help?"

Alex rested his hands on his hips. "Where were you Wednesday night—approximately four days ago—between the hours of nine pm to nine in the morning?"

Carl swallowed hard. "Um...Wednesday night? Well, I had dinner with a friend at her house, and then afterward we watched some TV and strategized about my farm. Things we could do to expand it and bring in more revenue."

"Who was this friend?" Alex asked.

Carl's eyes flickered to his house. "Do I have to say? I mean, it's no big deal. We're just friends, but I don't want Darsha to know." He held up his hands. "Just friends right now."

"Sheriff Stone and I saw you talking to Felicity Howler right before the fireworks started," I said. "You two looked pretty cozy. What were you talking about?"

A flush spread up Carl's neck and into his cheeks. "Oh, you saw that?" He kicked at some dirt under his feet. "Okay. So I've been sort of seeing Felicity. It really did just start out as me seeking advice about the farm. But the more time we spend together, the more I like her."

"So you were with Felicity Wednesday night?" Alex asked.

"Yes."

"At her place?" I asked.

"Yes. Until maybe around ten or eleven. I know I was home before midnight, because I keep the same curfew as my daughter."

I smiled. "Nice."

Carl grinned. "It's true. I wouldn't ask her to do anything I wouldn't do." He shrugged. "So I was with Felicity part of the night, and then I came home. Darsha went out with some friends for dinner, but she was already home when I got home. I went into her room, checked on her, and then went to bed."

"Just one more question," Alex said. "How long have you lived on Enchanted Island?"

Carl frowned. "Oh, wow. I don't know. Maybe about fifteen or so years now. Maybe a little longer? I honestly can't remember. Darsha was just a little girl."

"Why Enchanted Island?" Alex asked. "Do you have family here?"

"Not really. As a vampire supernatural, I pretty much have always known about Enchanted Island. When my wife died—a hit-and-run accident where they never found the driver—I decided Darsha and I needed a new start." He shrugged and spread his arms wide. "So I bought this place, we moved to the island, and we've finally turned it into what I have always wanted."

"Thank you for your time, Mr. Feeder," Alex said. "That's all the questions we have right now."

Deadly Caramel

Carl nodded, slapped his hat on his head, and smiled. "I better run and see to Darsha. You know the way out?"

Alex nodded. "We do. Have a good day."

"Same to you two."

I watched him jog off toward his house as I slowly made my way back to the Bronco. As I went to climb in the driver's side, my foot slid in a patch of mud.

"I got mud over here," I said. "Could be the mud we found in Hildegard's house."

"Think you can surreptitiously gather up a sample?"

Snorting at such a ridiculous question, I opened my door, swiped my hand in the air and levitated an evidence bag out of my kit, bent down and scooped up a small sample, then sealed the bag.

"Done," I said. "Now, let's go see what Felicity has to say about Hildegard *and* her budding romance with Carl Feeder."

Chapter 13

Felicity Howler lived on the edge of town near her family's landscaping company. Most of her brothers and sisters worked the business—except for Darren, who was still on the mainland. Even a couple of the married-in husbands and wives worked for Howler Landscaping.

"It's a cute house," I said as I parked in the driveway and shut off my Bronco. "Not at all what I expected."

Alex grinned. "I figured it had to be nicely landscaped, seeing as that's the family business."

"Yeah, but the cohesiveness of the landscape with the French country cottage look was a surprise for me."

I walked up the multi-colored cobblestone sidewalk, knocked on the pale blue door, then rang the doorbell just to make sure. While I waited for Felicity to answer, I stepped back and looked at the house again. The pale blue shutters not only matched the door, but it also brought out the blue-gray in the roof tiles. The cobblestone exterior was the color of warm, dry sand. Add in the amazing landscaping around the house, and Felicity Howler had made a nice home for herself.

The front door opened, and Felicity stood in running shorts and tank top, hair piled on her head, earbuds in, and sweat sliding down her temple. She yanked out one wireless earbud. "Now what? I told you everything I knew last night."

"Sorry to bother you," I said, "but we have a few more questions."

"C'mon in. I was just finishing up outside in my garden. I came in to get a drink of lemonade from the refrigerator and saw you pull in."

"You have a beautiful home," I said. "I love the colors and feel of the cottage."

Genuine pleasure and surprise crossed her face as she took out the other earbud. "Thanks. I've worked hard to get it this way. You guys want some lemonade too?"

"That would be nice," I said.

Alex and I followed her into the kitchen, neither saying anything as she pulled out a pitcher of lemonade from the refrigerator and filled three glasses with ice. She'd just handed us the drinks when a massive bark came from outside. I looked over and laughed at the black nose pressed against the glass-sliding door.

"That's Bingo," Felicity said. "He's a Great Pyrenees."

"That's a massive dog," Alex said.

Felicity opened the door and Bingo trotted in, pushed his nose against me, which caused me to stumble backward, and then waddled over to the kitchen tile and plopped down. His giant white body took up a huge section of the kitchen.

"I thought I was getting a cute little white, fluffy dog," Felicity said. "Joke was on me."

"How much does he weigh?" Alex asked.

"About one-fifty."

I laughed. "That's no little white, fluffy dog."

I closed my eyes and called silently to the dog, trying to home in on his emotions. I'd recently met a dog, Sassy, who could actually verbally communicate with me. I was eager to see if it would work with Bingo.

Deadly Caramel

Bingo whined, lifted his head off the ground, and gave me a puzzled look. He blinked a couple more times before letting out a little bark, causing his fluffy tail to thump loudly on the kitchen tile floor. He gave me what passed for a doggie grin before sprawling back down on the floor.

"What was that about?" Felicity asked.

"I can sometimes communicate with animals and plants," I explained. "Sometimes in actual verbal speech, but often just with emotions."

"That is so amazing," she said.

"Bingo seems to be very happy here," I said.

"I'm glad to hear that." Felicity reached down and gave Bingo a vigorous body shake before taking a sip of her lemonade and motioning for us to sit at the table. "Now, what's up?"

Alex set his glass on the table. "I take it you haven't spoken to Carl Feeder or anyone else today?"

Felicity's brows grew together. "Carl? No. But like I said, I've been in my garden most of the morning with my earbuds in. I don't even know where my cell phone is."

As if on cue, a whistle permeated the air, and we all turned to look at the cell phone sitting on the kitchen counter.

"That's my text notification," Felicity said. "Annoying, but I hear it." She got up to retrieve her phone. "Wow, I have like six missed texts."

"Why don't I tell you what's going on," Alex said. "This morning, Shayla and I stopped by to talk with Hildegard Broomington. Her name was given as a witch known to have access to the Sleeping Beauty Spell."

Deadly Caramel

"Okay." Felicity sat down at the table and set her phone away from her. "And what did she say?"

"Nothing," Alex said. "When we got there, her front door was open. Shayla and I discovered Hildegard on the third floor. Dead. It looked like someone hit her over the head and killed her."

"What?" Felicity's cry was so loud and shrill, Bingo lifted his head off the floor and whimpered. "You're wrong. You have to be. Hildegard isn't dead."

"I'm afraid she is," Alex said. "Doc Drago has already been called to the scene, and I have notified her son about what we discovered."

Felicity clasped her hands over her mouth and just stared at the two of us. She slowly lowered her hands and shook her head. "Isaac is going to be devastated. He and Hildegard are so close. I just can't believe this."

"When was the last time you saw Hildegard alive?" Alex asked.

"What?" Felicity shook her head. "Sorry. Um, I guess Tuesday. I clean her house on Tuesday evenings. Usually start after work around four in the afternoon and clean until seven."

"And you did this five days ago?" Alex asked.

"Yeah. I was there Tuesday, cleaned, and then left. She said she'd see me next Tuesday. She wasn't sure if she was feeling up to going to the July Jubilee. So she said if she didn't see me, she wished me good luck."

"What about Wednesday night?" Alex said. "Where were you Wednesday night from about nine at night to nine in the morning?"

Deadly Caramel

"Well, since you mentioned already speaking to Carl Feeder, I guess you know where I was. Carl and I were having a—well, a business meeting, I guess, here at my house."

I barely refrained from snickering at that.

"Actually," I said, "we know where you were until maybe eleven that night. Where were you after that?"

"Since we were at my house," Felicity said, "I just went straight to bed."

Alex nodded. "Okay. And how long would you say you've been seeing Carl Feeder on a personal level?"

Felicity's mouth dropped. "How did you know? Did he tell you? We've been so careful."

"And why's that?" I asked. "Why keep your relationship a secret?"

"He doesn't want his daughter to know yet. He asked to take it slow." She shrugged. "Even though her mom died when she was young, Carl never dated another woman."

"Darsha's twenty," Alex pointed out.

Felicity sighed. "I know. I don't totally understand it, either. But I want to give him his space to work it out."

I took a sip of my lemonade. "So what were you two really whispering about last night during the fireworks?"

Felicity blushed. "You saw us? We were setting up a time to meet today. I'm supposed to go out to his farm and pick up some fruit around three. He said his daughter is meeting up with some friends and hanging with them for an hour or two. So the coast is clear for us to see each other a couple hours later on." She ran her hands over her face. "I still can't believe Hildegard is dead. Murdered."

Deadly Caramel

Bingo stood up and pushed his head against Felicity's knee. She reached down absentmindedly and ran her fingers through his thick fur, a faraway look in her eyes.

"Felicity?" I said, calling her back to the present. "Did you ever go up to the third floor in Hildegard's room where she practiced her craft?"

"No. That was the only room off limits for me to clean."

"Did you ever see inside it?" I asked. "Do you know what was in there?"

"No. It was always locked." Felicity shrugged. "Truth is, for months when I started cleaning for her, she would get upset when I went to the third floor even just to vacuum. I finally told her if it made her feel safe—even though I knew she probably warded the room—she could just lock the room and wear the key around her neck so she wouldn't lose it."

I nodded. "Good advice. What about visitors? Did Hildegard have many visitors while you were there cleaning her house?"

Felicity frowned. "Whaddya mean?"

"I mean, while you cleaned her house, did she ever have company who came over to see her?"

"I guess so," Felicity said. "You mean like her son and daughter-in-law?"

"Yes," I said. "Like that. Or maybe friends?"

"Well, like I said, her son and daughter-in-law would sometimes come over for supper while I was cleaning. And another friend of hers would sometimes drop by to chat her up."

Alex shifted in his chair. "Do you know this friend's name?"

75

Deadly Caramel

"It's an odd name." Felicity smiled faintly. "Like Hildegard Broomington isn't, right? But this was another odd name. Latisha or Lorisha or something like that."

"Latrisha Wartski?" I asked.

"Yeah. That sounds about right. Older woman, just like Hildegard. Latrisha's niece or great-niece drives her over." She looked at me. "You'd probably know her. The niece is one of the competitors in the baking contest."

"Wendy Wand?" I mused.

Felicity nodded. "Yeah. We've talked a few times when she visits. I think I asked her what she was making, that kind of thing. Just casual like." Felicity closed her eyes and reached down to stroke Bingo's fur. "I hope Hildegard didn't suffer. She didn't deserve to die, but I hope she didn't suffer."

Chapter 14

"That was hard," I said. "She seemed to be genuinely sad about Hildegard."

Alex nodded. "She did. But killers can sometimes have remorse for what they've done. I don't think we can rule her out just yet."

"I know. I didn't see any mud in her yard or driveway, so that might be a plus."

"We didn't get a look at her garden," Alex said.

"Crap. You're right."

Alex opened the passenger-side door. "I received a text from Grant while we were questioning Felicity. He said the background checks on Wendy, Felicity, and Carl have come back. Nothing major stood out, but I told him we'd go to the station after talking to Wendy Wand and have a debriefing. You okay with that?"

"Yeah. We can drop off the mud sample while we're there so Finn can get a start on it tomorrow morning."

I pulled out of the driveway and laughed as my stomach rumbled. "You got any food at the station?"

"Frozen burritos, chips, and a couple other snacks."

"Good enough."

Wendy Wand lived in a subdivision on Fairie Lane near the fire station. Her home was a simple one-story bungalow with a detached garage.

Since she was a fellow witch, Alex decided I should take the lead. I knocked on the front door, and a few seconds later, Wendy stood in the doorway, a broom and dustpan in her hands.

"Good afternoon, Shayla. Sheriff, good to see you."

"Hello, Wendy," I said. "Can we come in and ask a few questions?"

Wendy hesitated for a fraction of a second before giving herself a little shake. "Of course. Please, come in. I was just sweeping my entryway. Would you like something to drink?"

I shook my head. "No, thanks. We just came from Felicity's place, and we had something there."

Hissing sounds stopped me in my tracks. I looked down and saw two pairs of blue eyes staring up at me, their backs arched, and their mouths open. "Jeepers!"

Wendy smirked. "Edwina and Eclipse. My Siamese familiars. So loyal to me. That's enough, you two. Go run along and play."

The two cats continued to hiss at me for another five seconds before both stopped, turned around, and sashayed out of the room.

"Let's just sit here in the living room then," Wendy said, motioning for us to take a seat on the couch.

"I'll get right to it," I said, eager to be away from the two hissing spitfires. "Do you know Hildegard Broomington?"

"Of course. She's friends with Aunt Latrisha, who is my great-aunt."

"Have you heard from your great-aunt today?" I asked.

Panic flashed in Wendy's eyes. "No. Is something wrong with Aunt Latrisha?"

Alex leaned forward on the couch. "I'm sorry to inform you, Wendy, but Hildegard Broomington was found murdered in her home this morning."

"What?" Wendy stood up from her chair. "Are you certain? How? I need to call Aunt Latrisha."

Alex and I both stood when she jumped up.

"I'm going to ask you to wait," Alex said. "We need to ask you some questions. We won't keep you long, but I really must insist you hold off calling your aunt until we finish here."

Wendy scowled, but quickly sat back down. "What do you need to know?"

Alex and I both sat back down on the couch.

"First," I said, "have you ever been to Hildegard Broomington's house?"

"Yes, of course I have. Aunt Latrisha and Hildegard are friends, and I often drive my aunt places because she doesn't have a license anymore."

"Last night," I continued, "GiGi told us three families were tasked to keep the Sleeping Beauty Spell safe and in their Shadows books after it was banned hundreds of years ago. Those modern descendants are now GiGi, Latrisha Wartski, and Hildegard Broomington. Did you know this story?"

Wendy shrugged. "Of course I knew this story. My aunt and I are close."

"Would you also agree," I continued, "if a witch got her hands on one of those very old Book of Shadows, a not-so-powerful witch might suddenly find herself capable of doing all sorts of spells?"

Wendy narrowed her eyes. "Are you going someplace with this?" She gave a small laugh. "What? You think I stole Aunt Latrisha's books? Trust me, she'd notice."

Deadly Caramel

I shook my head. "I don't think you stole Latrisha's Book of Shadows at all." I leaned forward and cocked my head to the side. "When Hildegard Broomington was found murdered this morning, her Book of Shadows was gone. Along with other books in her library."

Wendy's eyes went wide and again she stood. "You're accusing me of *murdering* Hildegard Broomington and then *stealing* her Book of Shadows? Are you insane?"

Once again, hissing sounds had me looking toward the hallway where the two demons known as Edwina and Eclipse sat and stared and hissed.

"Please sit down, Ms. Wand," Alex said.

Wendy's lips pursed, and her chest heaved up and down for two breaths before she finally sat, crossed her legs, and crossed her arms over her chest. "Fine. I'm sitting." Without a word, Wendy thrust one hand in the air, and the two cats crossed the room in three strides and leaped onto Wendy's lap. She stroked each one simultaneously. "There. That's much better. Please continue, Sheriff."

I tried to open a connection with the cats. But the more I tried to open the connection, the more push back I got. Those cats wanted nothing to do with me.

"I have just a couple questions for you," Alex said, as though nothing weird was going on in front of him with Wendy and her creepy cats, "and then we'll get out of your hair. First, you told Shayla and me last night that you never went back to the judge's table once you set down your lemon bars. But this morning, I was shown a timestamped photo of you at the judge's table around five-forty. Care to explain?"

Deadly Caramel

Wendy shrugged. "I don't know. I guess maybe I was earlier than I thought. I didn't realize it was that much earlier than the others arrived. After I watched the Wee Witches competition, I headed to the judge's table. I strolled by it to make sure everything looked good." She paused and scratched a cat's head. "I didn't realize I was that early. It was an honest mistake. After looking over everything and making sure my lemon bars looked delightful, I just stood off to the side. Soon, you all came over and things went crazy."

"Okay," Alex said. "When was the last time you saw Hildegard alive?"

Wendy snorted. "How am I supposed to know?" One of the cats curled up in her lap while the other one draped itself half on Wendy's shoulder, half on the top of the chair. "Maybe a month ago? I don't know."

"You haven't been out to see her recently?" Alex asked. "You go out with your aunt sometimes, right?"

"Yes, but I haven't done that in months."

"One last question," Alex said. "Where were you Wednesday night from nine pm until nine the next morning?"

Wendy threw up her hands and laughed, causing the two cats to open their eyes and hiss. "Seriously? How do I know off the top of my head? That was like *days* ago."

"It's okay," Alex said. "Take all the time you need. Four days ago."

Wendy sighed, closed her eyes, and started muttering to herself. I caught bits and pieces of shopping, visiting friends, watching a tv show on a certain night. Finally, she opened her eyes.

81

"I think Wednesday night after dinner, I just stayed in and watched TV. I usually try and go to bed around nine. I work about four days a week as a medical biller."

"You had no one over?" Alex asked. "You were alone the entire time?"

"Yes, Sheriff. I was alone. I don't just let anyone sleep in my bed."

I bit back a smile and kept my mouth shut. No sense getting a lecture on being snarky while on the job. The spray of water hitting a nearby window had the three of us turning to stare, and the cats hissing again.

"Be careful on your way out," Wendy said. "My automatic sprinklers are going."

Alex stood, and I followed suit.

"Thank you for your time," he said. "I'm sorry for your loss. I know you and your aunt were friends with Hildegard."

Wendy shook her head as she absentmindedly stroked the cat on her lap. "It's still so surreal. Poor Aunt Latrisha is going to be devastated."

"We'll see ourselves out," Alex said. "I know you're anxious to speak to your aunt."

"Yes, thank you."

I closed the front door behind me and watched the sprinklers shoot out water for a few seconds. It was peaceful to watch and listen to. Closing my eyes, I opened myself up to the surrounding flowers and smiled. They, too, were enjoying their bath.

"Everything okay?" Alex asked.

I opened my eyes and nodded. "Yes. It just gives me a burst of energy when I tap into the emotions of the surrounding plants. I tried to link with the cats inside, but I got nothing."

"I still can't get over that," Alex said. "C'mon, let's head to the station. I'm hungry."

"I got a better idea. Let's see what Mom has in her refrigerator. I guarantee she has better than frozen burritos. Plus, I want to let her know about Hildegard."

I stepped down off the walkway and noticed I'd stepped in mud. Not wanting to draw attention to myself—and just in case Wendy was looking out a window—I opened my driver's side door and levitated an evidence bag to me. Hoping it would look like I was trying to scrape mud off my shoe if anyone saw, I bent down and pushed a dollop of mud inside the baggie.

I jumped up inside my Bronco, lifted the evidence bag with mud in the air, and smiled. "Got us another sample."

Chapter 15

Mom was putting away the last of her lunch when Alex and I walked into her kitchen.

"Well, if this isn't a wonderful surprise," Mom said. "Can I get you guys some lunch? GiGi's in the bathroom, but we just had soup and sandwiches."

"Just sandwiches," I said. "We need to get back to the station and collaborate with Grant."

Sassy, the Papillon rescue now living with Mom, popped her head up from her dog bed. *"Miss Shayla, it's nice to see you again."* She pranced over to where I sat, her ears flapping like a butterfly. *"I like it here. You were right. Did you bring Needles? I liked Needles."*

I chuckled at Sassy's enthusiasm. "Needles is with Alex's daughter. But I'll tell him you said hi."

"Thank you. Thank you. I better go rest up. Mom and I are playing catch in the backyard later."

Sassy pranced back over to her bed, plopped down, and closed her eyes.

"So things are going well with Sassy?" I mused.

"She's a great dog," Mom said.

GiGi strolled into the kitchen, her eyes zeroing in on me. "You any closer to finding out who hurt Tamara and who had access to the Sleeping Beauty Spell?"

"Actually," I said, "it's worse than we originally thought."

"Whaddya mean, Shayla?" GiGi demanded.

Deadly Caramel

"I'm afraid I have some bad news," I said. "It looks like someone killed Hildegard Broomington for her Shadows book that had the Sleeping Beauty Spell in it."

"No!" Mom cried.

"This is terrible." GiGi started to pace. "Someone killed Hildegard *and* the book containing the banned spell is gone too? What is happening to this island? We seem to have an increase in crime lately."

"Crime happens everywhere," Alex said. "It was only a matter of time before it took hold on Enchanted Island."

"Still doesn't make it easy to swallow," GiGi growled.

"I agree," Alex said kindly.

"How was she killed?" Mom asked. "Or can you tell us?"

Alex shook his head. "I can tell you that Hildegard was killed, and that Shayla and I are investigating. That's about all I can divulge right now."

Mom handed Alex and me each a sandwich. "So someone on the island has a powerful book in their possession. That book needs to be found quickly."

"I agree," I said. "We're looking for it and a couple other things too." I took a bite of my sandwich. "What can you two tell me about Wendy Wand? She seems to have a grudge against our family. Why is that?"

GiGi snorted. "The Wands have always wanted to yield more power on the island than they do. While they go back for generations, they aren't original founding members. Unlike Wendy's mom, who is part of the Wartski family and *is* a founding member. The Wands believe that association should yield them more power in the witch community."

Deadly Caramel

Mom handed me a bottled water. "Which is sort of what this big coven meeting coming up is going to address."

"What's that?" I asked. "What big coven meeting?"

"This whole mess with Tamara and the Sleeping Beauty Spell has caused quite a stir in the myriad covens on the island," GiGi said. "I was on the phone all night with other coven leaders. They believe there's too much of a gap now and not enough cohesiveness amongst the covens. And I think they're right. It used to be there was only one large coven, and then slowly over the decades, they just split apart. Now, we have at least five different covens I can think of off the top of my head."

"So what's the solution?" I asked.

"A call has gone out this morning to each coven," GiGi said. "One person from each coven will be elected to represent a coven board of sorts."

"When will the first coven board meet?" I asked.

"Probably not for weeks still," GiGi said. "The individual covens need to vote on their one representative, then all those witches will have to find a day to meet, make an agenda, and all that. So I'd say it's still weeks away. But at least plans have been made."

"I think it's a fabulous idea," Mom said. "I couldn't tell you right now who all is in the Young Adult witches' coven or the Midlifers witches' coven. I'm excited."

GiGi grunted. "We'll see." She took a drink of her tea. "I take it someone told Hildegard's son about his mom?"

"I did," Alex said.

I pushed my empty plate back. "Mom, do you or GiGi know why maybe one of the contestants might want to have hurt one of the judges?"

"Is that what you're thinking?" Mom asked. "Maybe Tamara wasn't supposed to get hurt, but one of the judges?" She pursed her lips. "Well, the only one I can think of would be Lanny Golden, and that's because of his job. But I don't know anything major that would cause one of them to murder or physically hurt him. Nothing in the gossip mill."

"Maybe something," GiGi said. "Remember a couple years ago when Wendy's dad, Wyatt, wanted to build an expansion onto his shop? He was denied permits and could never build. He was livid and even threatened Barney Golden a couple times in public."

"Who is Barney in relation to Lanny?" Alex asked.

"His older brother," GiGi said.

Mom nodded. "Barney has been in charge of permits for about thirty years now." She laughed. "Pretty much everyone on the island who has been denied permission to build has a bone to pick with Barney."

"You think Wendy would wait all this time to strike?" I asked. "That's calculating."

"Revenge," Alex said. "One of the major reasons for murder."

"I don't know about Felicity or Carl," GiGi said. "Could be they'd been denied a permit too, or maybe denied a loan from the bank. Most people think Lanny is the sole decision maker for loans, but it's the board, not Lanny."

"But when you're seeking revenge," I said, "Lanny is a good person to start with."

Deadly Caramel

"We better get back to work," Alex said. "Thank you for the sandwiches, Serenity."

Mom blushed. "Any time."

"If you want to ask Barney about Wendy," GiGi said, "remember it's Sunday afternoon. You'll find him hanging down at the Leprechaun Lodge near the south end of the island."

***

"Do you want to go talk to Barney Golden real quick?" I asked.

"Sure. I'll text Grant and tell him we're running a little late."

It took about ten minutes to reach the south side of the island, where the Lucky Leprechaun was located. As Alex and I walked in, a round of groans greeted us—save the one lone "whoohoo" from the old guy at the bar.

Puzzled, I walked to the bar where a five-foot nothing woman with long black hair pulled up in a messy bun and sporting numerous tattoos stood wiping down the counter.

"Pay them no attention," she said in a voice that sounded like she gargled with gravel every morning. "Here at the Lucky Leprechaun we bet on everything."

I watched as one-by-one leprechauns got up from their seats and dropped a poker chip onto a nearby table under "man" or "woman" or "both" and received a piece of paper from the guy manning the table.

"Whatever sex walks through the door next," the barkeeper said, "declares the winner. If you win, you hand in

Deadly Caramel

your receipt and the winners split the pot. At the end of the night, whenever I decide to declare last call, whoever has the most coins wins a free beer. After that last haul Marvin just stole for betting both sexes, I'm sure I'll be buying Marvin a beer tonight." She winked at Alex. "Not real gamblin', Sheriff, since we don't bet with money."

I could tell by the frown on Alex's face he wasn't so sure.

"Name's Dakota," she said. "What can I get ya? I assume you aren't here to drink since you are both neither leprechauns nor members. So what'll it be?"

"We're looking for Barney Golden," I said.

"Barney? What's the po-po want with Barney? He's a good guy."

When Alex and I said nothing, she sighed and jerked her head to the right. "He's over in the back corner booth."

I thanked her and followed behind Alex as he ambled over to where Barney and another guy sat nursing a beer.

"Barney Golden?" Alex asked.

"That's me."

I guessed him to be in his late fifties, wavy ginger hair cut close to his scalp with threads of silver woven throughout, black-framed glasses, and more faded freckles than I could count.

"Am I in trouble?" he asked.

Alex chuckled. "Should you be?"

Barney grinned, showing off a dimple. I found him charming, but a lot of leprechauns were.

"I gotta run," his companion said. "We'll talk later, Barn."

Deadly Caramel

After the man left, Alex and I slid into the vacant bench across from Barney. Barney took a long swallow of his beer, set it down, picked up a coin, and started flipping it between his fingers. "What's up?"

"My name is Sheriff Stone, and this is Agent Loci," Alex said. "We'd like to ask you a couple questions about what happened yesterday at the July Jubilee. Did you hear about the young woman who was spelled with a caramel?"

"I did. My brother called to tell me about it. I was at the Jubilee, I just didn't see it happen."

"The more we're discovering about what happened, the more we're leaning on maybe one of the judges being the intended target. I've been recently made aware that Wendy Wand's dad had a beef with you a year or two back. Something about denied permits for an expansion?"

Barney stopped flipping the coin and frowned. "Yeah. That's right. He was pretty angry, we exchanged words, he continued to threaten me. I finally had to call Sheriff Hawkins and ask him to talk to Wyatt and get him to calm down."

"Did anything ever come of it?" Alex asked. "The threats, I mean."

Barney shrugged. "Nah. After a while he simmered down."

"What about Felicity Howler or Carl Feeder?" I asked. "Have you had an occasion to maybe have a run-in with either of them?"

"You thinking that maybe one of the contestants tried to poison Lanny to get revenge on me?" Barney asked. "That seems a little far-fetched, don't you think?"

Deadly Caramel

"Just covering all our bases," Alex said. "What about the other two? Have you had words with Felicity or Carl?"

"Not really," Barney said. "I mean, over the years with the Howlers, maybe. In fact, I'm pretty sure I have. You don't have my job for thirty years and not make enemies. But I can't see Felicity trying to hurt Lanny because I maybe didn't give her family a permit they wanted."

"But you'd say at least Wendy Wand and Felicity Howler may have had an issue with you at some time?"

"I guess at some time, yes."

"But not Carl?" I asked.

"Not that I can think of," he said.

"Thank you for your time," Alex said. "Have a good day."

Neither of us said a word until we were back in the Bronco.

"So," I said, pulling out of the parking lot, "Wendy and Felicity both may have a grudge against Lanny because of his brother. It's a better motive than we had yesterday."

"True. Let's head to the station and put this all together."

Deadly Caramel

Chapter 16

The coroner, IT guy, and forensic technician all had their labs in the basement of the sheriff's station. It was a small department, but the equipment was new and the workers were brilliant and dedicated. They were a tight-knit group held together by an eighty-year-old witch named Pearl who sat behind the desk. Pearl's twin sister, Opal, ran the upstairs sheriff's department with the same tight-fisted control Pearl did.

I was genuinely surprised to see the desk empty. Pearl once told me if any of her staff was on call, she was on call.

"Wonder why Pearl isn't here?" I mused.

Alex chuckled. "Same reason why you won't find Opal upstairs today."

I raised an eyebrow at him. "And why's that?"

We headed down the hallway toward Doc Drago's lab.

"Because our delightful twin sisters are on a picnic with—and I'm quoting here—'potential suitors.'" He shot me a grin. "Yeah, you heard me right. The spinster sisters have snagged two potential suitors for themselves. And get this..." He stopped and leaned down until his breath caressed my ear, making me shiver. "Our girls are cougars! These boys are only seventy-five."

"What?" I demanded. "Who?"

Alex laughed, straightened, and continued down the hallway. "You're never going to believe the story I got."

"Tell me!" I demanded as we stopped in front of Doc's door. "I can't believe you've known something juicy like this and not said anything!"

Deadly Caramel

"Herb and Basil Caraway," Alex said. "They moved to the island three months ago when their one-hundred-year-old mother passed away. They are known as the Caraway Twins."

"Caraway? Are they kitchen witches?" I asked.

"I believe so."

"Herb and Basil?" I laughed. "That's the funniest thing I've heard in ages! Can you imagine if things work out for them? The Earthly sisters will marry the Caraway brothers. I like it."

Alex knocked twice on Doc's door, then pushed it open. "Doc? You in here?"

On the other side of the sterile room, Doc Drago looked up from the body on the table. "Perfect timing." He stood, took off his gloves, and motioned for us. "Please come in and take a look at what I've found."

Dead bodies don't bother me. Dead bodies cut up...not my most favorite thing. But I had a job to do, so I needed to witch up, pull on my big-girl panties, and go have a look. Luckily, when we got close, he turned and walked us to his computer.

"I just plugged everything into the computer to generate a report. I found wooden slivers in her head wound. Also present were microscopic red paint chips."

I frowned. "Wooden weapon that's red? So a red baseball bat?"

Doc shook his head. "No. The weapon is thinner than a bat."

"So a red wooden stick or dowel?" Alex mused.

"Something like that," Doc agreed.

I gasped. "Like a broom handle?"

Alex snapped his fingers and nodded. "Good thinking! I know the broom and dustpan I have at my house are red."

"Are we back to circling around Felicity as the killer?" I asked. "Housekeeper would probably have access to a broom."

Alex frowned. "It would *seem* like we should focus our attention that way, doesn't it? But I believe my set is red."

"Mine too," Doc added.

I nodded. "When we saw Wendy today, she was sweeping her floors. She had a red broom. Now what?"

Alex smiled. "We see if we can eliminate the other two suspects."

"While the blow to the temple is what killed her," Doc said, "it wasn't the only thing odd I found. On her upper arm, I found what looks like an injection site."

"Injection site?" Alex mused. "You mean like someone tranqued her?"

Doc nodded grimly. "Looks that way. Probably a paralytic, but I'll have Finn run a tox report just to make sure."

"And all the bruises we saw on her?" I asked.

"Awful, aren't they?" Doc mused. "Take a look."

Stifling a groan, Alex and I went to stand on one side of the table across from Doc.

"She's still wearing the key," I blurted.

Doc nodded. "Yes. I'm afraid it must be warded or spelled, because it can't be removed from around her neck."

"And the bruising?" Alex asked.

Deadly Caramel

"Perimortem." Doc pointed at the body. "You can see from the bruising around her ribcage and chest here that the killer probably dragged her up the stairs." He stepped down to Hildegard's lower extremities and lifted one leg. "See here. Bruising on back of both calves. Consistent with being dragged up the stairs and her legs hitting the steps."

"That's just awful." I quickly blinked back the tears I felt stinging my eyes. I'd cry *after* we got the killer.

"It *is* awful," Doc agreed. "And someone needs to pay for what they did to her."

"Agreed." Alex stepped back from the table. "Thanks, Doc, for getting this to us as fast as you did. I really appreciate it."

Doc's eyes filled with sorrow. "I'm sorry for Hildegard. She didn't deserve to go out like she did. Sweet old girl that she was."

"I have some samples of mud for Finn," I said. "I'll just run them over to her lab and leave a note."

"I'll do that for you," Doc said. "Just leave them here with me, and I'll make sure she gets them in the morning. I'll need to talk with her about the tox report and everything anyway."

"Thanks." I handed him the two samples I collected. "Hopefully she can let us know if there's anything that stands out."

We said goodbye to Doc and headed upstairs to the sheriff's station. Grant was sitting at his desk looking over paperwork and eating peanuts.

"Hey, boss." He motioned to the papers on his desk. "Got those backgrounds you wanted. I'm also going over notes I took last night from the three judges, plus the interview I had this morning with Latrisha Wartski."

"Then let's hash this out," Alex said as he and I sat down in the empty chairs Grant had set out for us. "Tell us about your interview with Latrisha."

"I interviewed her earlier this morning, before you informed me about Hildegard. Anyway, I asked her if her family had access to the Sleeping Beauty Spell, and she said yes, but the book the spell was contained in was locked away in a safe in one of her rooms. I asked to see it, and she was able to show it to me. I then asked her if anyone—her niece included—had approached her recently and asked to be shown the spell. She said no to both questions."

I leaned forward in my seat. "Did she say anything about the Sleeping Beauty Spell?"

"Interestingly enough," Grant said, "she was *not* at the July Jubilee due to health reasons, so she hadn't heard about what happened to Tamara. When I informed her, she was shocked. She said there's no way that could have happened, unless someone got their hands on the Sleeping Beauty Spell, and if it wasn't hers, then it had to be either Hildegard Broomington or Matilda Witchman." He chuckled. "I had to ask who Matilda Witchman was, because I'd never heard that name before."

I grinned. "Yeah, GiGi rarely uses her given name, so you have to know her pretty well to know her real name."

"Or her last name," Grant continued. "It took me by surprise I didn't know her last name, either."

I shrugged. "She's just GiGi to everyone on the island."

Deadly Caramel

"I'm curious," Alex said, "of the two witches she named, did she intimate which one might have given it out?"

Grant shook his head. "Not at all. She was pretty adamant that neither woman would ever let the spell be shown, just like she wouldn't."

"Interesting," Alex said. "Especially when you think about the fact that two contestants in the contest had relatives with access to the spell—a very secretive and dangerous spell."

"I really didn't get any pertinent information from her," Grant said. "When we ended the conversation, she did say she would call Hildegard and see what she had to say."

"Which would be nothing," I said. "She was already dead a couple days."

"This can't be about the bake-off itself, right?" Grant asked. "I mean, there's no monetary exchange given to the winner, right?"

"Right," I said.

Alex crossed his arms over his chest. "We know Tamara ate the caramel and was harmed, but I think we can all agree she was not the intended target."

"I agree," I said.

"Ditto," Grant added. "The killer had no way of knowing who would eat the caramel. It could have just as easily been one of the judges."

"Which is what I think *should* have happened," I said. "Maybe the killer wanted to hurt one of the judges."

"Who are the judges again, Grant?" Alex asked.

"Selma Oakley, Trudy Bloodman, and Lanny Golden. Selma is a retired art teacher, Trudy owns Enchanted

Treasures Bookstore, and Lanny is a loan officer at Enchanted Island First National."

I snorted. "Lanny is going to *love* hearing from us after our last run-in with him."

"What did backgrounds tell us?" Alex asked.

Grant handed me then Alex a copy of his report. "Not much. Wendy Wand has never been arrested, but she has tons of outstanding speeding tickets. Felicity Howler is in the same boat. No arrests, but she has a drunk and disorderly charge against her. Years ago, though."

I laughed. "I remember Mom telling me about that."

"What happened?" Alex mused.

"I hadn't been gone from the island long," I said. "So Felicity was probably around twenty-five. One night she went for a run in her werewolf form along the beach. No big deal. Except when she shifted back to human form, she stayed on the beach and consumed quite a bit of alcohol from what Mom said. She was so drunk, she started shifting back and forth and howling at the moon. One of the selkies finally ended up calling Sheriff Hawkins." I laughed. "He ended up having to arrest her because she was so drunk...and naked. But it obviously got pleaded down."

Alex smiled. "Thanks. Now every time I see her, I'm going to be thinking about that."

Grant laughed. "I get it, though. I sometimes feel like doing the same thing she did on full moon nights after a good run."

"And Carl Feeder?" Alex asked.

"Misdemeanor protest charges," Grant said. "Lots of those. And that's both when he lived on the mainland and some since living here on Enchanted Island."

"What would he protest here?" I asked.

"Anything and everything," Grant said. "In fact, his daughter, Darsha, even has a misdemeanor charge against her. I contacted Sheriff Hawkins to see if he remembers Darsha and her dad getting arrested, and Hawkins said Darsha was getting picked up with her dad since she was a little girl. It was never anything major—protested local candy store for using red dye, Enchanted Island Café for serving sugary soft drinks to kids—that kind of thing. So Hawkins just took the dad in, dad paid the fine, no big deal. Darsha would sit on the waiting bench against that wall over there and wait until her dad was released."

"I can see Carl doing that," I said.

"But when Darsha turned eighteen," Grant continued, "Hawkins said he couldn't turn a blind eye anymore. Which was perfectly fine with Darsha, evidently. She was excited the first time she was arrested with her dad." Grant shrugged. "Seemed harmless enough. The last major arrest was one year ago, right before I came on the job. I guess Dad and daughter were arrested for protesting at the local laundromat for not offering organic laundry soap."

I laughed. "Again, I can see that."

"Still," Alex said, "there's nothing that stands out. No assault and battery, nothing violent in any of the backgrounds. So let's look at judges. We have a retired art teacher, bookstore owner, and a loan officer. Just going by that, I'd say we look at the loan officer. Are any of our suspects being forced to sell their property? Do any of them have large outstanding loans?"

"That's a great question to ask Lanny," I said. "We'll have to wait until tomorrow when the bank opens. But even if they have large loans, killing Lanny won't matter."

Alex looked at his watch. "We've been going since early this morning. It's nearing five. I say we call it a day. Deputy Sparks is out on patrol right now, and he still has a few more hours. I'll call him and see if he can go to Felicity's and Carl's houses and see if they will willingly show us their brooms." He turned to me. "Saves us from having to run around and do that tomorrow."

"Sounds good." I stood and stretched. "I think we accomplished quite a bit today."

Grant stood up from behind his desk. "I'm going for a run tonight with Dash Stryker. He's still shattered about his brother's arrest for murder back in February. So I'm trying to help him keep it together."

"Enjoy your run," Alex said. "We'll talk tomorrow."

Deadly Caramel

Chapter 17

"Hmm," Alex said when I pulled into his driveway. "I see Brick is here. How am I supposed to feel about this?"

I laughed. "Needles is inside. I'm sure you have *nothing* to worry about."

He chuckled. "You're probably right. And I knew this day was bound to happen, where I'd be replaced by another boy, but it still hurts."

I bit back a smile because I knew he was being serious. "I'm sure you haven't been replaced. Just like I'm sure you have nothing to worry about with Needles inside."

"You coming in?" he asked.

"Chicken."

He let out a bark of laughter. "Yes, I am."

We let ourselves inside...and were greeted by silence.

"I don't like this," Alex said. "I thought I'd have more time before I had to give her the 'no boys allowed in your room' speech. If I look like I'm going to go for my weapon, hold me back."

Grinning, I gave him a thumbs-up sign. What I didn't tell him was that from my vantage point I could see not only into the kitchen, but through one of the windows into the backyard. I could see Zoie and Brick were outside.

"Where is Needles when I need him?" Alex demanded. "And I can't believe those words just came out of my mouth!"

This time I did laugh. "You need to calm down. It looks like everyone is in the backyard."

"The backyard?" Relief sagged his shoulders. "Of course. Why didn't I think of that?"

Deadly Caramel

I bit back the retort that was on my tongue. No sense adding to his Dad stress.

I followed Alex as he practically sprinted through the house and into the backyard. He threw the back door open so hard, I was afraid it would fly off the hinge.

"Hey, Dad!" Zoie waved a softball in her hand. "Brick and I are playing keep-away from Needles. Wanna join?"

Because Alex still had that wild-eyed look on his face, I slid my hand up his back for comfort before stepping around him.

I made eye contact with Needles and could swear the sneaky little porcupine was smirking. "You ready to go?"

"I'm rather enjoying the gargoyle's unease," Needles said.

Zoie and I both laughed.

"We are out of here," I said. "Zoie and Brick, thank you for your help today."

"No problem," Brick said.

"Are you staying in town?" Alex asked.

I shook my head. "I need to go tell Dad about Hildegard."

"Right." Alex tugged me back inside the house, then wrapped his arms around my waist. "If I'm saying goodbye now, I don't want to do it outside in front of everyone."

I grinned and wrapped my arms around his neck. "Is that so?"

He leaned down and kissed me. And for a few minutes, I put everything from this morning aside and just focused on the two of us. Something I didn't do often enough.

Deadly Caramel

When he finally released me, and I opened my eyes...I caught the flutter of wings out of the corner of my eye. Turning my head, I groaned. Sure enough, Needles was peeking in through the window.

"I guess I should go." I leaned up on my tiptoes and gave Alex a quick kiss. "I'll text you tonight before I go to bed."

Alex raised an eyebrow. "That's a long way off. You *sure* you are going straight home, Loci?"

I grinned. "Of course, Sheriff Stone. Where else would I go?"

A few minutes later, I was back behind the wheel of my Bronco with Needles snuggled in the back. I pulled out my cell and called Serena's number.

"You busy?" I asked when she picked up the call.

"Not really," Serena said. "Tamara is staying with her mom tonight. Grant is going for a run and spending some time with Dash Stryker, so it's just me and the kitties at home."

"Speaking of kitties," I said, "I have an errand I'd like to run and need a distraction. Care to go?"

"Heck yeah. Pick me up soon?"

"Ten minutes. Oh, and bring some of your goodies you always have on hand."

I hung up and grinned over my shoulder at Needles. "Let's go on a fact-finding mission."

Needles' wings fluttered. *"Excellent idea, Princess. Where are we going, and what's my job?"*

***

Deadly Caramel

"Why do I have to be the cat distracter?" Needles whined.

"Because I sure the heck ain't gonna be the cat distracter," I said.

Serena chuckled. "How bad can these cats be?"

I shuddered. "You have no idea. It was creepy the way they flanked Wendy, draped over her, stared and hissed at me. Animals usually love me and enjoy communicating with me."

"What exactly is the plan or the goal?" Serena asked.

The three of us got out of the Bronco and headed toward Wendy's front door.

"Needles, hide under my hair and my shirt collar," I said, taking down my ponytail and giving my thick mane a fluff. "I don't want Wendy or the cats seeing you just yet."

"So degrading," Needles sniffed as he gently landed on my shoulder, folded his wings, and burrowed under my hair. *"I'm a soldier, not a nursemaid."*

I rolled my eyes.

"Let me guess," Serena whispered. "He's not happy?"

"Nope," I said. "Basically Needles is going to keep the cats distracted, you are going to chat up Wendy, and I'm going to look for Hildegard's Book of Shadows. We know it's missing, and last night at the judge's table, Wendy made some off-hand comment about how she's had a little extra help this year, and so there's no way she can lose. That sounds pretty suspicious to me."

Serena rang the doorbell while I scoped out the house better. Since it was one story, there weren't many hiding places she could have the book...either still in the kitchen from when she made the caramel or in an extra bedroom where she probably performed her spells and practiced her craft. All I had to do was get in the bedroom without the cats discovering me.

"I'd say this is a surprise," Wendy said dryly, "but I'd be lying. If you are here to snoop around for Hildegard's Book of Shadows, let me save you the trouble. I don't have it."

"Shayla stopped by my house to tell me about Hildegard, and I wanted to offer my condolences to you and your great-aunt." Serena handed her a plate of assorted cookies. "I've been trying new recipes and thought you might enjoy them."

Wendy suspiciously eyed the plate for a few seconds before grabbing it, stepping back, and motioning us in. Eclipse and Edwina stood in the small entranceway, staring me down. They both hissed, and I wondered if they smelled Needles.

"They're looking at me like I'm their personal catnip toy," Needles hissed in my ear.

I brought up the rear as we walked into a sunny kitchen. Splashes of red and yellow stood out against the white walls and cabinets. Copper pots hung from a rack above her stove, and little pots of herbs were tucked away in every nook and cranny.

"It's a nice space," I said. "Cheery and functional."

"Thank you." Her crisp tone let me know she really didn't care what I thought. "Suits me fine. I suppose I should offer you some tea or coffee."

"Hot tea would be great," Serena said.

Deadly Caramel

Sighing, Wendy set the plate of cookies on the counter and busied herself making tea. When she set the kettle on the burner, I figured that was my cue.

"Could I use your bathroom?" I asked.

Wendy's look all but burned holes through me. "You aren't going to find Hildegard's Book of Shadows hiding in a bedroom, so why bother looking?"

I cleared my throat. "I'm sure I wouldn't. I really am just asking to use your bathroom."

Wendy nodded her head to Eclipse and Edwina, and the two cats fell into step with her as she ushered me down a hall. I looked over my shoulder at Serena. She was giving me big, scared eyes. I couldn't say I blamed her.

"It's down this hall," Wendy said when we came to a "t" in the hallway. "Second door on the right. Eclipse and Edwina will stand guard and keep you company."

"That's just weird," Needles said.

"Thank you, Wendy," I said, ignoring Needles. "I shouldn't be long."

"See that you aren't."

The minute she passed me in the hall, I sprinted to the second door on the right. Sure enough, it was the bathroom. Peaking over my shoulder, I wasn't surprised to see the two Siamese cats glaring at me.

I opened the closed door next to the bathroom. "You take this one."

Needles flew out from under my hair and zipped into the bedroom. I quickly closed the door as the two cats hissed and sprinted down the hall. I opened the door directly across the hall on the left, leaped inside, and closed the door behind me. It was Wendy's spell room. Luckily, there was still enough daylight outside I didn't have to turn on a light.

With a wave of my hand, I magically opened the hutch drawers against one wall. After a quick peek, I came up empty. There were at least fifty books lined up neatly on her bookshelf, and nestled in a small cradle was a large leather-bound Grimoire…not Hildegard's Book of Shadows.

A thump, followed by a hiss and loud screeching had me running to the door. I flung it open and stepped out into the hallway as Needles made a beeline for the safety of my hair. He'd just gathered in his wings and slipped down the back of my collar when Wendy came careening around the corner.

"What is going on back here?" she demanded.

I looked down at the hissing and screeching cats as they leaped in the air. I knew they were trying to find Needles, but I played it cool. "I was coming out of the bathroom when Eclipse and Edwina attacked me. The only thing I can think of is that they smell other animals on me. You know, since I *am* the game warden."

Wendy narrowed her eyes. "I don't believe that for one minute." She snapped her fingers. "Eclipse! Edwina! Stop that right now." The two cats stopped hissing and screeching, but they didn't stop swiping their paws at me.

I tried to hop over the two cats as gracefully as I could, but I knew I looked ridiculous. "I guess this proves I need to wash my uniform tonight."

"I take it you're satisfied?" Wendy asked.

"What?" I knew my innocent look wasn't fooling her.

Deadly Caramel

"Are you satisfied that you didn't find Hildegard's Book of Shadows in my spell room?"

"I don't know what you're talking about, Wendy." I hurried past her and practically ran into the kitchen, where Serena sat spellbound. "Have you finished your tea, Serena?"

Serena nodded and set her cup on the table. "Oh, yes."

"Then I guess you two can leave," Wendy said.

"Enjoy the cookies," Serena called over her shoulder as I dragged her from the kitchen, through the living room, and out the front door...the hissing cats trailing after me the whole way.

As we hopped up in the Bronco, we dissolved into a flood of giggles.

"What the heck went on back there?" Serena demanded. "All of a sudden we heard the most insane noises coming from the other side of the house. Wendy practically flew through the air she was running so fast!"

"Those cats are freaky," I said. "For some reason, I can't tap into their ability to communicate."

Needles popped out from under my hair. *"Those weren't cats, they were baby demons with claws. If I didn't dislike them so much, I'd say they'd make great bodyguards like me."*

That caused me to laugh even harder.

I was about to tell Serena what Needles had said when my cell phone rang. "It's Alex." I put him on speakerphone. "What's up?"

"I just got a call from Deputy Sparks," he said. "Felicity and Carl both admitted to having a red broom. Carl could produce his, but Felicity couldn't."

Deadly Caramel

"You're kidding!" I gasped.

"Nope. Sparks is bringing Felicity in right now for me to question. I know you're probably minutes from home, but do you want to sit in?"

"You and I both know I'm nowhere near home," I said. "I'll be there in fifteen minutes."

Deadly Caramel

Chapter 18

By the time I dropped Serena off at her place and hauled butt to the station, I had three minutes to spare. Needles was still snuggled up and resting in the crook of my neck, his wings brushing over me with each breath he took.

Grant and Sparks looked up from their desks when I barreled inside the station. "You staying around too, Grant?"

"Oh, yeah. I already called and let Serena know." He grinned. "Oddly, she didn't seem the least bit surprised."

"Hmm, that *is* odd." I wasn't going to admit to anything. "Must be a witchy thing."

Alex snorted as he closed the door to the interview room. "Must be none of us are dumb enough to think you went straight home without making a pit stop to pick up Serena for a stakeout somewhere."

Needles perked up at Alex's tone, zipped out from his sleeping spot, and shook a paw at him. *"Talk to my princess in that manner again, Gargoyle, and I'll snap off your stone wings!"*

Grant laughed. "No idea what Needles just said, but I'd say you aren't his favorite person, Sheriff."

"Has she lawyered up?" I asked, hoping to change the subject.

"Nope," Alex said. "She still maintains someone stole the broom out of her work van."

"Convenient." I sent Alex a grin when Needles went back to snuggling against my neck.

"I'm getting Felicity some coffee," Alex said. "If you guys want to watch in the observation room, go for it."

Deadly Caramel

A few minutes later, standing behind the one-way mirror, Grant, Officer Sparks, and I watched as Alex reentered the room and set a cup of doctored coffee in front of a crying Felicity.

"Let's pick up where we left off," Alex said. "You admit you use a red broom when you clean houses?"

"Yes." She took a sip of the coffee. "I keep all my cleaning supplies in the Howler Landscaping van I use to get around in."

"That would be one of your dad's company vans?" Alex asked.

"Yes. I keep a broom, mop, vacuum, and various other cleaning supplies on hand at all times."

"And tonight, when Deputy Sparks asked to see your red broom, you could not produce it, correct?"

Felicity wiped her eyes. "That's right. But I swear it was back there the last time I checked."

"Which was when?" he asked.

"Let me see." She closed her eyes, counted under her breath, then opened them. "I know for a fact I saw it Wednesday morning. I remember because it had rolled to a different spot while I was driving, and I needed to move it back where it belonged."

"You don't remember seeing it Thursday?" Alex prompted.

Felicity shook her head. "No. So someone must have stolen it out of my van Wednesday sometime."

I turned to Grant. "We *do* know the time of death was Wednesday night."

"I guess it's plausible," Grant murmured.

I turned back to the glass and watched Alex.

"Do you keep your van in your garage or in your driveway?" Alex asked.

"In my driveway."

"And is it always locked?" he asked.

"No! No, it's not." Felicity leaned forward. "I hardly ever lock it. I mean, it's Enchanted Island. Nothing ever—well, okay, recently some bad things have happened, but usually nothing bad ever happens here. I don't lock my car or my house, normally."

Alex arched an eyebrow. "You may want to rethink that if you believe someone stole the murder weapon from your van."

Felicity gasped. "So you're sure my red broom is the murder weapon?"

"Well," Alex drawled, "when we finally find your red broom, I believe we'll have no problem matching the weapon to what killed Hildegard."

"Oh, gosh!" Felicity buried her head in her hands and sobbed quietly. "I don't understand what's going on."

"Felicity." Alex waited until she raised her head. "We know you have access to Hildegard's house, and tomorrow, Shayla and I are going to talk with Lanny Golden, one of the judges in the bake-off. When we ask him if he's recently had any contact with you, what do you think he'll say?"

"No." Felicity shook her head back and forth. "I mean, he'll say yes, but how would I even know which judge would eat the spelled caramel?"

"What did you speak to Lanny Golden about?"

Deadly Caramel

Felicity sighed. "I wanted to take out a loan from the bank. I went to see Lanny about two weeks ago to see about securing the money. He called me Tuesday afternoon and said no to the loan. Right now I have too much debt on my house. But he swore, as soon as I could get it down, he'd have no problem securing the loan for me." She wiped at the tears spilling down her cheeks. "But it's no big deal. I went to the bank because I didn't want to go to my dad. But I've already decided to swallow my pride and ask Dad for a loan."

Alex leaned forward and looked Felicity in the eye. "If you need to tell me something before things get too far out of control, like me reading you your rights and then having everything on record, you need to tell me now."

"I don't understand any of this."

Alex sighed. "Felicity Howler, did you take Hildegard's Book of Shadows from her spell room after you hit her over the head with the broom and killed her?"

"No! I *swear!* Please, I'll do anything! Check my house. You can go there right now! You won't find anything because I have nothing to hide!"

"You are giving the Enchanted Island Sheriff's Department permission to enter your home and search for the murder weapon *and* Hildegard's Book of Shadows?"

"Yes! Please, Sheriff. Please look everywhere. I promise you, I didn't do this."

Alex stood. "I'd like to go right now, and for you to accompany us. Is that okay with you?"

Felicity stood. "Yes, of course."

"Wait right here, please."

Deadly Caramel

Alex exited the room, and a few seconds later, the door to the observation room opened. "Well, who's going?"

Grant and I both shot our hands in the air.

Alex chuckled. "I figured as much."

"I'll stay and man the phones," Sparks said. "Good luck."

***

Felicity hadn't been lying about not locking her house. The four of us—with Needles hovering above my shoulder—ambled up her walkway and straight into her home. Bingo galloped into the foyer, then slid to a halt when he saw a roomful of people...I could sense his apprehension. He let out a little bark, but Felicity quickly quieted him.

"This is Bingo," she said to Grant. "Probably a major reason why I don't lock my doors."

"He's beautiful." Grant gave Bingo a couple scratches before turning to Alex. "Where do you want me to start?"

"You check the garage," Alex said. "I'll check inside here. Felicity, I noticed a shed out back when we were here before. Would it be okay if Shayla checked it?"

"Of course. I have nothing to hide."

Needles and I headed out the kitchen's back door, stepped out onto the deck, down the wooden stairs, and across the cobblestone pavers to the shed. There wasn't a ward preventing me from going inside, so I waved my hand in front of the door and stepped into darkness.

"Where are those annoying fireflies when you need them?" Needles snickered.

I conjured up a light orb and tossed it in the air, illuminating the inside of the shed. There was a push mower and weed eater to the left, a pegboard filled with gardening tools directly in front of me, and to the right was a row of shelves crammed with watering cans, bags of compost, gas cans, and tons of other outdoor items.

And propped up in the right-hand corner of the shed was a broken red broom handle in front of a white plastic bag that I was sure held Hildegard's Book of Shadows.

"Looks pretty damning," Needles said.

"But why not hide it better?" I asked. "It's basically out in plain sight."

"Think I could borrow that stick real quick and give the gargoyle a little love tap?" Needles asked, his wings turning a yellow-green. *"Might be pretty entertaining."*

"Behave." Sighing, I snapped on a glove from my back pocket, bent down and moved the broom handle out of my way, and carefully opened the plastic bag. An old leather-bound book the size of a large laptop computer peeked up at me. "I don't want to open the book here. But I think we definitely have enough to arrest Felicity. Needles, can you get them?"

With a jaunty salute, Needles zipped out of the shed, while I stood and looked around. The orb's light let me see everything easily enough. There wasn't a single item out of place. Even the cement floor was clean. If someone other than Felicity *had* entered the shed, there was no way to tell. If the ground had been dirt, I could have maybe gotten a footprint...as it was, nothing stood out as being off.

Deadly Caramel

"What did you find?" Alex demanded as he stepped inside the shed. "Needles came barreling inside the house, gesturing, wings all glowing. I figured that meant something."

Without saying a word, I pointed to the corner. Grant and Felicity stood in the shed's doorway, Needles hovering behind them. Everyone looked to where I pointed.

"I don't know how that got there!" Felicity gasped. "I mean, I was just in here this morning working on my garden. Remember? It wasn't there. Trust me, I would have seen it."

"I'll process the scene and gather the evidence," Grant said.

Sighing, Alex whipped out his handcuffs from his belt. "Felicity Howler, you're under arrest for the murder of Hildegard Broomington and the attempted murder of Tamara Gardener. Anything you say can and will be held..."

Alex's voice trailed off as he led a weeping Felicity out of the shed.

Deadly Caramel

Chapter 19

I pulled up to Enchanted Bakery & Brew the next morning, already exhausted. After Felicity was booked into holding, her lawyer called, and everything settled down, it was pushing eight-thirty. The thirty-minute drive home did nothing to settle my nerves. I still had a few questions I needed Felicity to answer for me. Foregoing my normal run to see Dad, I dragged myself up the stairs and dropped into bed. Unfortunately, I woke up around two and tossed and turned the rest of the night.

I needed coffee in the worst possible way.

As I walked into the bakery, Alex pulled up behind my Bronco and parked. I held the door open for him as he jogged over to me. Giving me a quick kiss, he breezed past me in the door.

"You're looking tired, Loci," he noted.

"Bite me," I tossed back good-naturedly.

Needles zipped in from the outside, quill in hand. *"How dare he insult you, Princess. I'll cut out his tongue and feed it to the dog outside!"*

Zoie let out a bark of laughter from behind the display case. "Oh, Needles. You're so funny!"

"What did he say?" Alex grumbled.

"Nothing," I said. "Just Needles being Needles."

"How's Tamara?" Alex asked Serena.

"Good. She should be back at work tomorrow."

I looked at Zoie, who avoided eye contact with me. "How are you feeling, Zoie?"

"Good," Zoie quickly said.

117

"Why wouldn't she be feeling well?" Alex asked.

I narrowed my eyes at Zoie. "You haven't said anything?"

"Said what?" Alex asked. "What am I missing?"

Zoie sighed. "Nothing, Dad. I just haven't been feeling well lately."

"Whaddya mean?" he demanded. "What's wrong?"

"Nothing!" Zoie scowled at me, but I didn't let her anger bother me. "Sometimes I just don't feel well. It's nothing to worry about. I'm a growing girl. These things happen."

Alex furrowed his brows. "If you say so."

"I do," Zoie insisted.

Needles flew down and landed on my shoulder. *"I think I will stay here and watch over Miss Zoie, if that is okay with you?"*

"I would appreciate it, Needles."

We ordered two cinnamon rolls, two coffees, and paid Serena. With a wave goodbye to not only Serena and Zoie, but to other patrons in the bakery, we headed outside to Alex's vehicle.

"I've been thinking." I clicked my safety belt. "I'm not one hundred percent sure about Felicity's guilt."

Alex started the engine and pulled out onto the street. "I got that last night when you didn't call your ex-partner at the Paranormal Apprehension and Detention Agency to come get her."

I turned in my seat to face him. "Do you think Carl is setting her up? I mean, he was at Felicity's house Wednesday night. Do you think he stole the broom when he said goodnight to her, went to Hildegard's house and killed her, and then brought it back sometime Sunday to Felicity's to frame her?"

"I don't know," Alex said. "I guess anything is possible. But why? What motive or possible reason would Carl have to kill Hildegard and poison one of the judges? And why frame the woman he supposedly cares about?"

"I think it's time to pay Lanny Golden a visit," I said. "Maybe he can shed some light on all this."

Enchanted Island First National was on the corner of Charm Street and Cherry Tree Lane, just a few streets down from the bakery. I opened the door and strode inside, Alex right on my heels. I hadn't been inside the bank since our last run-in with Lanny. I didn't figure this talk would go any better than our previous one had months back.

Lanny must have felt my gaze, because he looked up from his desk and caught my eyes through his office window. He didn't even try to suppress his grimace. Standing, he motioned us over.

"I figured you'd stop and talk to me eventually," he said when we entered his office.

"We won't take up much time," Alex said. "We just have a few questions."

Lanny sighed and sat down. "I hope this ends better than the last time."

"I'm sorry about your friends," I said quietly.

"Thank you." He motioned for us to sit. "Now, what questions can I answer for you? I assume this is about the attempted—what? Is it considered murder?"

"Yes." Alex leaned forward in his chair. "As I'm sure you're aware, we are trying to pin down who and why our suspects from the bake-off would want one of the judges dead. When looking at the three judges, you are the one that stands out." Alex looked around the office. "In your line of work, I'm sure you've had your fair share of upset clients."

Lanny held up his hand. "I know what you're asking. And we go a long way here at First National to protect our customers. So I can't—"

"It's a murder investigation," I said. "You also need to remember that this could have ended in *you* being the victim of the Sleeping Beauty Spell. Not Tamara, but you."

"All we are asking you to do is to think about the three other competitors in the bake-off," Alex said casually. "Felicity Howler, Wendy Wand, and Carl Feeder. Which of those suspects, if any, have you recently had an altercation with? Maybe turned down for a loan? Maybe was threatened by one?"

Lanny shook his head. "It really wasn't like that." He sighed. "It's a small island, and word is out. Everyone knows you guys arrested Felicity last night. I know you're wanting me to confirm for you I had this big showdown with Ms. Howler, and that's why she wanted me dead. Only I can't. What I can tell you is that Felicity came to me a few weeks ago about a loan. After looking over her finances, the bank board voted to turn her down. *Right now.* And I stressed those exact words to her. At this time, the bank couldn't justify loaning her more money. However, when she paid down what she owed, we'd have no problem loaning her more. She's a wonderful and loyal customer."

Alex nodded. "And the other two names? Any contact with them recently?"

Deadly Caramel

"No. Wendy Wand doesn't even bank here."

"And the other name?" I asked.

"I can't tell you anything," Lanny said.

I had to wonder if it was can't tell us or won't tell us. There was a huge difference.

"Thank you for speaking to us." Alex stood, and I followed suit. "Hopefully we will have this case wrapped up quickly, and you can rest easy."

Lanny sighed. "I just *hate* this about Felicity. I mean, she's always been a loyal customer here at the bank, and she's always been pleasant to me anytime I saw her." He ran his hands over his face. "But, then again, I don't seem to be the best judge of character. I didn't realize two of my best friends were killers until I was almost framed."

Alex shook Lanny's hand. "Don't be too hard on yourself. Thanks again for speaking with us."

I gave him a small wave and led the way out of his office, across the lobby, and out the front door to the Blazer. I waved hello to Mrs. Mystic and her horde of kids, hopped up inside the vehicle, and buckled my seatbelt.

I waited to speak until Alex got in. "He gave us what we needed. Confirmed what Felicity told us last night. Felicity applied for and was denied a loan. That could be a solid enough motive to kill someone. Plus, we have what we believe to be the murder weapon used to kill Hildegard Broomington from Felicity's shed in her backyard. We also have the Book of Shadows taken from Hildegard's home, which was also found in Felicity's shed." I snorted. "I mean, it's a slam-dunk now, right?"

Deadly Caramel

Before Alex could answer, his cellphone rang. He put it on speakerphone. "This is Sheriff Stone."

"Hey, Sheriff. It's Finn. I have results back from the tox report I ran early this morning from Hildegard Broomington. I show trace amounts of strychnine in Hildegard's body."

"Strychnine?" I mused.

Alex's brow furrowed. "Hey, Finn. Do you know if there are any plants that produce strychnine?"

"Plants?" Finn mused. "Let's see. Off the top of my head, I'd say yes. I believe that falls in the gelsemium genus, and those would include flowers like yellow jasmine."

I gaped at Alex. "And you're thinking a landscaper might have access to that plant, aren't you?"

"I am," Alex said. "Thanks, Finn."

"No problem, Sheriff. When I have the results back from the mud I'm analyzing, I'll ring you back. Also, nothing unusual came back from the other desserts on the judge's table. All just basic ingredients."

"Good to know," I said.

"One last thing," Finn continued, "I analyzed the paint chips from the broom handle, and Doc and I both agree that the broom handle is the murder weapon. Everything is a match, from the actual size of the weapon to the paint chips found in the wound."

"Thanks, Finn," Alex said. "Good work."

Alex disconnected the call.

I shrugged. "So this pretty much proves Felicity is the killer."

Deadly Caramel

Chapter 20

"I guess it does," Alex agreed. "I've been dodging calls from Carl Feeder all night and morning. I think we owe it to him to go out and talk with him real quick."

"Okay."

Alex started the Blazer, and my cell phone rang.

"It's Mom." I put her on speakerphone. "Hey, Mom. What's up?"

"I may have something for you regarding Felicity and her finances," Mom said. "It might go to motive."

It was on the tip of my tongue to tell her Lanny already confirmed she was turned down for a loan, but I let Mom speak.

"Margie Lightbird told me she was at Cup Up and Dye a few weeks back getting her hair done," Mom said. "While there, she overheard one of the hairdressers comment about Carl Feeder expanding his business. Maybe taking on a partner. The feedback was mostly joking because while Carl's veggies are amazing, no one really expects him to go anywhere with his organic produce and eggs and—well, his overall lifestyle."

My heart sank, and I looked dejectedly at Alex. "Thanks, Mom. That actually helps."

"Happy to be of service. You two stay safe today."

I disconnected the call. "So Carl asked Felicity to invest in his farm. When Felicity was turned down for the loan, she decided to get revenge. I guess once we confirm with Carl we know he was thinking of bringing on Felicity as a partner, I can call my ex-partner. There's no denying Felicity is the killer."

"I'm sorry," Alex said. "I really am. I can tell you're taking this hard."

I threw up my hands. "I am. And I have no idea why. I mean, Felicity has never been a fan of Tamara's. She's always been a little mean to her because of what happened with her brother, Warren. You think I'd be happy to get her away from here." I shrugged. "But I'm not. And I don't know if it's because I've gotten to know her as an adult supernatural, and I find I like her. Or if it's something more that's not sitting right with me."

"Let's go talk with Carl," Alex said. "Maybe then you'll feel better about Felicity's guilt."

He turned left at the corner to head out of town, when his cell phone rang.

"It's like Grand Central Station," I joked.

Chuckling, Alex put his phone on speakerphone. "This is Sheriff Stone."

"Hey, Alex. It's Serena."

Alex's eyes met mine, and I saw the flash of panic and worry. "What's up? Everything okay?"

"Actually, it's Zoie. I don't think she's feeling well. Could you stop by the bakery sometime and maybe check on her? See if you want me to take her to the doctors? I know you guys are super busy today."

"Be there in two minutes," Alex said.

We pulled up to the bakery in less than one minute, and Alex was out of the vehicle the second he put it in park. I followed close on his heels as he charged into the bakery. A few heads turned our way as we hurried over to where Zoie sat, her head resting on a table.

"She's had some water," Serena said from behind the counter. "I told her to rest until you got here."

Zoie opened her eyes and lifted her head. "Hi, Dad. Hi, Shayla."

"What's the matter?" Alex demanded. "Why didn't you tell me you weren't feeling well this morning?"

Zoie sighed. "Because you go all 'Crazy Dad' on me anytime I say I'm not feeling well."

Alex's head snapped back. "I do not."

"My sympathies, Miss Zoie," Needles said as he zipped over and landed on the table, his wings a shimmery blue. *"I can totally see the gargoyle doing just that."*

"Besides," Zoie continued, after giving Needles a little smile, "I don't know exactly what's wrong, so I don't know what to say."

"What *is* wrong?" I asked as I sat down, then motioned for Alex to do the same when he remained standing.

"Oh, right." Alex sat down and took Zoie's hand in his. "What exactly is wrong?"

Zoe shrugged. "Same symptoms I've been having since my birthday. Queasy insides. Sometimes it feels like my heart is going to leap out of my chest."

"Anxiety?" Alex asked. "If it is, it's perfectly understandable, Zoie. We *did* just move to a new area—heck, a whole new world in many ways. You started a new school, you just turned sixteen."

"You started honing your skill as a witch," I added. "And in doing so, you've put a lot of undue stress on yourself to learn as much as you can in a short amount of time."

"True," Zoie said.

"You were granted the ability to hear and understand me." Needles grinned and did a little twirl. *"But I can't imagine that would have anything to do with stress."*

Zoie and I both laughed out loud.

"What did I miss?" Alex asked.

"Nothing," I said. "All of these are new experiences, and they can be overwhelming."

"I guess that could be it," Zoie admitted. "Now I feel silly for Serena having called you guys, especially when you're right in the middle of a big investigation."

Alex wrapped his arm around her shoulder and gave her a side hug. "Don't ever feel silly about asking for help, Zoie. I'm your dad. That's sort of my job."

"And I'm your friend," I added. "That's sort of my job."

Zoie grinned. "So does this mean I get to tag along today?" She sobered. "Because I really don't want to be alone. I still feel a little off."

I looked at Alex and shrugged. "We're pretty much done."

"Don't see why not, baby girl." He drew her to him and kissed her forehead. "I'm just glad you opened up about what's going on."

Deadly Caramel

Chapter 21

Alex had just turned off Enchanted Way Road and was about to pull into Feeder Farms when his cell rang. I saw it was Finn and put her on speakerphone.

"Sheriff Stone," Alex said.

"Hey, Sheriff. I finally got the mud sample analyzed from the crime scene. On top of standard mud, there was trace amounts of—and I'm not kidding here—poop found in the mud. And, yep, you heard that right. Poop."

I looked toward the enormous area where the chickens had free rein on Carl's farm. "Not surprising."

"When I analyzed the other two samples you gave me, only one had the same components. It's the sample of mud from Carl Feeder's farm. Hope this helps."

"It does," Alex said. "Thanks for getting to those samples so quickly."

I disconnected the call and turned to Alex. "Last nail in the coffin. We know Felicity is secretly dating Carl, and she comes out here quite a bit."

"We do?" Zoie piped up from the back.

"Actually," Alex said, his voice reverberating slightly as he drove over the cattle guards in Carl's driveway, "we might have a problem."

I frowned. "What kind of problem? This pretty much ties my hands. I have no choice but to call my ex-partner immediately."

"Think about it, Shayla." Alex glanced over at me. "We know on Tuesday that Felicity was at work landscaping all day, then she went out to Hildegard's house to clean later that night. She admitted cleaning the hallway on the third floor, so yes she *was* up there, but what are the chances she tracked mud up there from Carl's farm, and it landed in the exact place where Hildegard would later be found?"

I frowned. "Slim. But we know Hildegard was killed Wednesday night, not Tuesday night."

"Exactly," Alex said as he drove past the main house out to the barn and veggie stand. "Felicity worked all day Wednesday landscaping, and then came home Wednesday night. Someone from Carl's farm broke into Hildegard's house *later* that night. Felicity was never at Carl's farm on Wednesday—he came to her. Again, what are the chances Felicity managed to somehow retain mud from Carl's farm on her shoes for who knows how many days, only to drop some next to the murder victim?"

"Slim to none," I whispered. "Which leaves us where?"

Alex pulled to a stop in front of the open barn. A huge closed sign covered the veggie stand. "Which leaves us in a dangerous place. It makes more sense that Carl had the mud on his shoes when he left his farm Wednesday night and drove out to Felicity's place for their date. After he leaves her house, he grabs the murder weapon out of the back of Felicity's van and drives to Hildegard's house. There must have been mud still left on his shoes." Alex shut off the engine. "Zoie, you don't even think to move from this car. Do you understand me?"

"But Dad, maybe I can—"

"No," Alex and I both cut her off.

Deadly Caramel

Needles flew to within an inch of Zoie's face, shook his head, and waggled a paw at her. *"Miss Zoie, you must stay here. Do not argue."*

Zoie rolled her eyes. "This is lame. I know magic. I can help."

"No." Alex unhooked his seatbelt. "We have no idea what we're even up against here. We just received new information that doesn't fit where it should. We are going in blind, and Shayla and I need our senses about us. We can't be worrying about you."

"Fine," Zoie said. "I understand. I don't like it, but I promise to stay here."

"Thank you." Alex turned to me. "You ready?"

I nodded. "I have my gun and my magic."

"I'm going to call Grant real quick for backup."

I waited until he'd hung up from Grant before firing my questions at him. "So we're thinking it's Carl? He set up Felicity? But why? What's the motive? What did he have to gain by poisoning the caramel? And how, exactly, did he manage that feat without being a witch? Does he have magical abilities? And then why—"

"I don't know." Alex interrupted me as he opened his door. "Let's go ask."

"We don't know where Darsha is," I cautioned as I gently pressed my door closed so it wouldn't make any noise. "Carl may have snapped and has her inside the barn."

"I'm aware," Alex said.

He unholstered his gun, but I preferred my magic in instances like this.

Alex stopped in front of the open doors. "Could be that's why the stand is closed. Darsha is inside. Proceed with caution."

We'd just stepped inside the dimly lit barn when we heard yelling toward the back of the barn. Alex motioned for me to take the right, and he covered left. From the way the hens were squawking, I didn't need to tap into their emotions to know they were upset.

I stopped in front of a bale of hay to listen in on what was going on. Out of the corner of my eye, I saw Alex doing the same thing on the other side of the barn. I gently nudged a hen aside when she tried to peck my leg and focused in on what the argument was about.

"I heard you talking to her a couple weeks ago about bringing her in as a partner."

"She will bring in revenue," Carl said. "And we need that. We need her investment. Plus, I *really* care about her. I *want* to make her a part of this team."

"This isn't *her* place," Darsha screamed. "It's *mine*! And I've done what I had to do to keep it that way."

Chapter 22

"My gosh, Darsha!" Carl cried. "What have you done?"

"I think you know," Darsha said.

"Are you saying *you* killed Hildegard?" Carl asked. "Is that why you're holding me hostage? But why? How did you even know about Hildegard and her powerful magic?"

"Do you *really* think I'm that stupid, Dad?" Darsha sneered. "I've known about you and Felicity Howler for months. Practically the entire time you thought you were sneaking around and then telling me you were just friends. I've been listening to your conversations. I know everything." She paused. "Speaking of knowing everything, why don't you two come on out? I know you're here, Sheriff. And I know you brought the witch with you."

"How does she know that?" I nearly screamed aloud as Needles dropped onto my shoulder. *"She's a vampire, not a witch."*

"What are you doing here?" I hissed. "You're supposed to be with Zoie."

"She's napping. She started to feel strange again, so she laid down and went to sleep."

"I said come out!" Darsha yelled. "If I have to do a reveal spell, I'm going to be pissed."

I nodded once to Alex across the barn as Needles hid under my hair and collar. Once he was settled, I raised my voice to be heard. "I'm coming out."

"Me too," Alex called.

"Nice and slow," Darsha said. "I've gone this far. I won't hesitate to shoot either one of you."

"What's gotten into you, Darsha?" Carl demanded. "I don't understand what's going on."

I stepped around the tall bale of hay and held my hands up for her to see. In truth, I didn't want to use magic on her until I had her confession and had a ton of questions answered. "I don't understand a lot of things, either."

"No sudden moves." Darsha waved the gun in her hand. "Where's the Sheriff?"

"Right here." Alex walked out from around the tractor. "Let's just take this nice and slow, Darsha. We can work this all out. No one else needs to get hurt."

"Please!" Darsha scoffed. "That ship already sailed, Sheriff. You and I both know it. I was just trying to cover my tracks real quick before you put two and two together and came looking for me. But I see I wasn't fast enough with my getaway."

My eyes flickered down to Carl, who was sitting stiffly in a chair. Every so often he tried to move, but couldn't. "Binding spell?"

Darsha grinned. "Yep. No matter how much he tries to move, he ain't going nowhere."

"How?" I asked, hoping to keep Darsha talking. I didn't want her thinking about the gun Alex still had on him. "How did you manage all this? You aren't a witch, you're a vampire. At least, that's what your dad indicated. How are you doing spells and working magic?"

"My mom was half witch and half vampire," Darsha said. "Bet you didn't know that? I was just a little girl when she died, so I didn't even know I could do magic until recently. But I'm resourceful. I've been secretly practicing for a year now once I realized I had magical abilities."

"Why didn't you ever say anything?" Carl asked. "I'd have supported you."

"At first I wanted to surprise you," Darsha said. "And then a few months later, when I realized your intentions with the farm, I decided I needed to use it to keep what was mine."

"What are you even talking about?" Carl demanded. "I don't understand."

"Of course you don't!" Darsha waved her gun precariously in the air. "You never listen to me."

"We're listening now," I said. "Tell us."

"I knew Felicity and my dad were getting tight. I just didn't realize until it was too late that Dad was thinking about bringing her, a complete *stranger*, into our business."

"It's not our—"

"No!" Darsha cried. "This is *my* time. I found out you were bringing her on a few weeks back when I overheard Felicity say she would try and get a loan at the bank. I knew then I had to do something. At first, I thought about just outright killing her, but I was afraid I might get caught. I needed to figure out a plan to either make her death look like an accident or do something bad and set her up to take the fall."

"Oh, Darsha." Carl closed his eyes and shook his head.

"Then you started talking about entering the baking contest," Darsha continued, "and how Felicity was also entering. When I found out one of the judges was going to be the loan guy at the bank…it was like it was kismet. I knew what I had to do." She shrugged. "Sort of. I just didn't know *how* to do it. Until last week, when Felicity was out here at the farm under the guise of buying blueberries, and you two sneaked off to do your thing. I followed you guys. I heard you ask to see her Tuesday, and she said she was cleaning Hildegard's house Tuesday evening, and she really needed to keep the schedule because Hildegard's son was out of town. She said she was really just checking up on the old witch, but you guys could get together Wednesday after work."

"And the strychnine?" I asked. "How did you know to do that?"

Darsha smirked. "Like I said, I've been studying up. I also know on this island pretty much every plant imaginable grows here. It was just a matter of finding the yellow jasmine and extracting the poison."

"Tell me about Wednesday night?" Alex coaxed. "How did that go down?"

Darsha shrugged. "About three months ago, Dad invited Felicity out for dinner. Just as friends, he said. Anyway, she got to talking about her side job of cleaning houses and mentioned how this one witch she cleans for is so strict, Felicity can't go in one of the rooms on the third floor because it's this woman's spell room. And just to make sure no one ever goes in it, the old witch keeps the key to the room around her neck at all times." Darsha tapped her temple with her index finger. "I stored that information up here. I don't know why. I just did."

"And so Wednesday night," I said, "after your dad left to go see Felicity, you went to Hildegard's?"

Deadly Caramel

Darsha shook her head. "No. I waited until Dad had been gone about fifteen minutes, followed him to Felicity's house, broke into her van, stole her broom, broke off the handle, *then* went to Hildegard's. When the old witch opened the door, I injected her with the strychnine."

I frowned and thought about the house. "Why did it look like there'd been a struggle in the foyer?"

Darsha's eyes flared with anger. "The witch surprised me! I figured once I slipped her the paralytic, she couldn't do any magic. I didn't realize she could still use her mind without saying the words."

I snorted. "I bet that took you by surprise."

"I said it did, didn't I?" Darsha took the gun off her dad and waved it in my direction. "But I guess you'd know that seeing as how you're supposed to be this big and bad witch yourself, right? I ought to just shoot you right here, right now. Then we'd see how big and bad you really are."

"Stop," Carl begged. "Please, Darsha."

Darsha brought the gun back to her dad's shoulder. "Anyway, like I said, it took me by surprise, but I have vampire speed, so it didn't take me long to subdue her. My other big surprise was that the damn key couldn't be removed from her neck! I guess she spelled it or something, because no matter how hard I pulled or what I tried, it wouldn't go over her head or yank off. So I adapted and dragged her body up the stairs, bent her so the key could be inserted in the lock, then once the door was open, I bashed her over the head with the broken broom handle."

"Then you callously walked over her dead body," I said, "and grabbed her Book of Shadows."

Deadly Caramel

"Damn right. I needed to make it look like Felicity stole it. Of course, I had *no* idea what a jackpot I'd find, though. I mean, I knew she was old and powerful...I just didn't realize *how* powerful. Imagine my surprise when I stumbled upon the Sleeping Beauty Spell with three days to spare before the bake-off." She smiled and shrugged. "I knew you guys were looking at Felicity for the murder of Hildegard—which was how I planned it—so I kept the murder weapon and Book of Shadows hidden, and then later planted them in Felicity's shed Sunday when I knew she would be here with Dad. I made a big deal to tell him Saturday at the festival I wouldn't be home during that time." She grinned. "I had to plant evidence."

I frowned. "Why didn't Bingo bark or attack when you stole the broom and later when you returned the book?"

"The huge dog?" Darsha mused. "Because I put a silencing spell in the peanut butter balls I threw to him. Once he gobbled them up, I had five minutes to do my thing." She smirked. "As you can see, it was meant to be."

"I'll tell you what's meant to be," Alex said, "and that's you behind bars for the rest of your life."

"Nice try, Sheriff." Darsha placed the gun next to her dad's temple. "But that's not going to happen. I'll admit, things aren't going to work out how I hoped. The plan was for *me* to take over this farm." She pressed down hard on her dad's shoulder with her free left hand. "This place was supposed to be *mine*. I was going to run this place."

Carl sighed. "You were never going to run this place anytime soon, Darsha. That's what you never understood. You always assumed you were entitled to what I'd built from the ground up. But you weren't. I didn't want my products changed. You did. Until I could get you to understand what I was trying to accomplish out here, you were never going to inherit."

"But it was *mine* to inherit!" Darsha exploded. "I have been out here helping you for years."

A massive noise overhead caused us all to look up.

And that's when Alex made his move.

It happened so fast…yet it felt like I watched it unfold in slow motion. Even Needles didn't react in time.

Deadly Caramel

Chapter 23

The barn roof crashed down around me, and a massive form dropped down in front of me. Alex whipped out his binder, but Darsha, who already had her gun out and ready, was faster. She pulled her trigger. The bullet raced my way. But instead of me taking a bullet to the chest...it ricocheted off the statue in front of me.

Alex's aim was true with the binder, and Darsha was surrounded by an invisible forcefield holding her hostage.

I blinked my eyes, trying to make sense of what I was seeing in front of me, while being vaguely aware of Carl on the ground weeping.

"Who? What?" I croaked.

"I don't know what's going on," the deep voice in front of me responded. "I'm so scared."

"It's Zoie," Needles said, his wings a dark purple. *"She's a gargoyle!"*

I heard Alex calling for an ambulance, and I told myself to pull it together. Now was not the time to fall apart. "Needles, stay with Zoie. I need to secure the scene."

"I got her, Princess."

I ran over to where Carl knelt on the floor, sobbing uncontrollably. Alex looked over at me, fear and rage warring in his eyes. "She was going to shoot you." He frowned. "She *did* shoot you."

"I know."

He turned and looked behind me...and his mouth dropped. "What? Is that *Zoie*?"

Deadly Caramel

"I think so," I whispered. "I'm not sure what's going on. I just wanted to make sure you had everything under control over here. Needles is with Zoie."

"How? How is she a gargoyle?" He took a step backward, and I reached out to steady him. "I thought she got all her mom's genes and was a witch? She's *never* had any gargoyle tendencies. This is crazy."

"We'll figure it out," I promised. "Right now, I need to call my ex-partner and get him to the island."

Alex tore his eyes from Zoie and nodded. "You're right. Let me take Carl. Can you see to Darsha? Grant should be here any minute now."

"Of course."

I shooed away a couple stray hens and stood back as Alex extracted a weeping Carl from the barn. I ignored the snarling Darsha as best I could. When Grant came charging into the barn, I motioned him over, and we started to process the scene.

Ten minutes later, the paramedics arrived. By this time, I had coaxed Zoie to shift back to her human form. It had taken a lot of tries, but she finally managed it.

"Why?" Zoie sobbed against my neck. "Why do I have to be a gargoyle? Did you see my hideous body? I'm huge and rocky and have claws for hands. And *wings*! Not the pretty kind, but ugly gray ones. I'm ugly!"

"Hey," I patted her back, "don't say that. Your dad is a gargoyle, and you think he's cool."

"But he's a *guy*," Zoie wailed. "It's okay for him to be all stony and huge and bulky. I'm a girl. I look like a freak! Did you hear my voice?"

Deadly Caramel

I pushed her off me, grabbed her shoulders, and looked her in the eyes. "What I saw and heard was a magnificent creature standing in front of me like a warrior goddess. One who took a bullet for me. If it weren't for you, Zoie, I'd be dead right now!"

She sniffed and frowned. "What? What're you talking about?"

"You don't know?" I demanded. "Zoie, when you landed in front of me, Darsha had a gun in her hand. You caused a distraction, your dad made his move, but Darsha pulled the trigger anyway. That bullet would have gone in my heart—killing me—had you not been standing in front of me as a gargoyle. You saved my life!"

"I did?" She sniffed again and smiled. "That's kinda cool."

"Kinda cool?" I laughed and yanked her to me, giving her a tight hug. "That's hella cool. You saved my life, Zoie. I'll never be able to thank you enough."

Zoie giggled. "Did you just say 'hella'? You are so weird sometimes, Shayla."

"Midlife does that to you sometimes," I joked.

She stepped back and grinned at me. "So I can stop a bullet? Dang. I guess that sort of makes up for the claws and deep voice. Maybe not so much the gross skin though."

"Plus, you can fly." I laughed. "Just don't remind your dad of that fact right now. He didn't want me teaching you how to levitate. This is going to make levitating look like you're sitting still."

"Yeah?" Zoie said. "Did you hear that, Needles? I can fly. Just like you!"

"We will need to have a race soon to see who is the fastest." He did a little twirl in the air, his wings shimmering green and yellow.

"You're on!" Zoie laughed.

"What's going on over here?" Alex asked as he ambled over to us. "How're you feeling, Zoie?"

"Can you believe it, Dad?" Zoie mused. "I mean, a *gargoyle*. Did you become a gargoyle and shift for the first time when you were sixteen? Why didn't you tell me this would happen?"

Alex hugged his daughter, then set her away from him. "I had no idea. Usually a gargoyle shifter is a gargoyle shifter. I think I shifted the first time when I was like eight or so. It's just always been a part of me. I don't understand what's going on, but we'll figure this out."

"When I go out to see my dad tonight," I said. "I'll ask Black Forest King if he knows why this has suddenly happened."

"It's sort of like Grant," Alex said. "He didn't shift into a werewolf until just recently when he moved to the island, correct? Maybe Zoie always had a dormant gargoyle gene that suddenly came to life when we moved here."

I nodded. "Makes sense. I can't wait to hear what Dad has to say."

"Until then," Alex said, "we have a lot of clean-up to do here. I called Deputy Sparks and told him to bring Felicity Howler out here. She may be able to help Carl. He's so grief-stricken right now. I want the paramedics to give him something, but he's refusing because it's not all natural."

"Let's see what Felicity can do for him first," I said. "Is Darsha still in the binder?"

"Yes," Alex said. "Gonna keep her there as long as possible." He sent me a grin. "She's not a happy camper."

"How are *you* doing?" I asked. "Knowing Zoie got shot and then finding out she's half gargoyle and half witch?"

Alex pressed his lips together and looked away. "Not good. You can't imagine the ache and fear that gripped my heart when I learned she'd been shot at."

Zoie reached out and hugged Alex. "I'm sorry you're hurting, Dad."

He dropped a kiss on the top of her head. "Thank you. Every time I think about the fact Darsha's bullet struck you, I am filled with terror. Absolute terror."

"If it will make you feel better," Zoie said, "I won't mention how cool it is that I can fly now."

Alex groaned. "My heart can't take much more."

Chapter 24

"Wow, Darsha Feeder was behind this all?" Serena mused once I finished telling the story. "I can't wrap my head around it. I mean, I didn't know her well, but a killer? Never saw that coming."

"Me neither," Tamara said.

By the time everything was wrapped up out at the Feeder Farm, it was almost three. Mom and Aunt Starla drove out to the farm to pick up Zoie and Needles and deposit them back at the bakery. Carl Feeder had been given a natural sedative by Mavis Gardener, Tamara's great-aunt who lived not far from the farm and who'd been called in special by Grant. Alex went back to the station to fill out forms and write his report on what had happened to give to the mayor. And I went straight to the bakery.

Serena topped off my coffee then sat back down at the table with Tamara, Zoie, Mom, GiGi, and me. Needles was curled up asleep against the napkin dispenser. "It basically sounds like Darsha felt she was entitled to run the farm and would do anything she could to make sure she kept control of it."

I nodded. "And yet it was never hers to begin with. I mean, Carl was excited at the possibility she may one day follow in his footsteps, but it was obvious they didn't agree on everything. And ultimately it was and still is Carl's farm. He can do with it whatever he wants. If he wanted to bring on a partner, then that was his right."

Zoie sighed and swirled her mocha. "And Darsha was selfish enough to make sure her dad didn't do that. She killed a defenseless older witch so she could frame a woman who—by all accounts—seems to love her dad, and did it all because she felt she was entitled to something that wasn't hers."

"That's about it," I agreed. "And then we had another huge surprise today."

Zoie laughed. "You mean me? Yeah, I'm still trying to wrap my mind around that." She sighed. "Brick asked me out."

My head snapped up at that. "What? That's awesome, Zoie. I really like him. In fact, I'm surprised he hasn't called me yet to get an interview."

"I *thought* it was awesome," Zoie said, "until I shifted. Now, I'm not so sure." Tears filled her eyes and slid down her cheeks. "What if I shift during our date? How is he going to handle that? I mean, I'm a *gargoyle*. It's not like I shift into something beautiful, like a mermaid or fox or something like that. I turn gray, my skin hardens, my voice deepens, my hands turn into claws, and wings spurt out of my back." She swiped at her face. "Nope. I'm going to cancel."

"No, you aren't." I laid my hand over hers. "You aren't being fair to Brick. You're assuming he won't be able to handle it because *you* aren't able to handle it right now. Give you both some time." I laughed and gave her hand a light squeeze. "I mean, seriously. The guy's name is Brick. He'll probably think it's cool his girlfriend can turn into a gargoyle."

"He's not my boyfriend!"

But I could tell by the pink that spread over her cheeks she wouldn't mind that happening.

Deadly Caramel

"I hate to run," I said, "but I need to tell Dad what all has happened."

Mom kissed my cheek. "Tell your dad I said hello."

GiGi snorted. "Tell your dad I said he's an—"

"That's enough." I held up my hand to stop whatever word was going to come out of GiGi's mouth.

GiGi grinned. "What?"

I reached down and gently scooped a snoring Needles up in my hands. "I'll talk to you guys later."

***

I hit my stride on the path and opened myself up to the surrounding forest. I left Needles at the castle, so I really wanted the lightning bugs to escort me. Not for the light—for it was still light outside—but for the company. And I wasn't disappointed.

"Princess, how is your friend feeling?"

"Black Forest King will be happy to see you!"

"When are you bringing Miss Zoie back out for a visit?"

Unlike Needles, I didn't tell them to scram...instead, I listened to their incessant chatter all the way to the entrance of Black Forest.

"Good evening, Mr. Pine," I said. "May I enter, please?"

"Always, Princess Shayla."

The pine tree lifted his heavy branch off the forest floor, and I scooted inside. Feeling a peace I hadn't felt in days, I hurried to my dad. Tonight, more than ever, I just wanted his comforting touch and soothing voice.

Soon the thick forest died away, and I stepped into the rolling green meadow where Dad lived. With a cry of joy, I jumped up on one of his roots and ran until I reached his trunk. Wrapping my arms around him, I hugged him as tightly as I could.

"Here now." I felt the light brush of leaves over my back as one of dad's branches caressed my back. *"What's this, Shayla? What's wrong?"*

Stepping back, I swiped at the tears that rolled down my cheeks. "So much has happened since we last spoke. I'm afraid I have bad news. Hildegard Broomington was murdered by a young woman who selfishly thought her dad owed her something. Her dad, Carl Feeder, is devastated by what she's done. My heart hurts for him and for the Broomington family."

"I am saddened by this news," Dad said. *"Nearly forty years have passed since I last spoke with Hildegard, but she will be missed. She helped me in a time when I needed it, and I will always be thankful to her for that."*

I sat down and leaned against his trunk. "That's nice to know."

"What else is on your mind, Daughter?"

I shook my head. "I still can't believe it. Right in the middle of capturing Darsha—the girl who killed Hildegard—Zoie came crashing through the roof of the barn. She'd turned into a *gargoyle*!" I turned and faced his trunk. "Dad, did you know that would happen?"

Dad said nothing for a few seconds.

"I wondered if maybe it would happen. It's like Serena's fiancé, whose werewolf gene was dormant. I

Deadly Caramel

wondered when I met Miss Zoie if perhaps her gargoyle gene was also dormant. Living on Enchanted Island affects some supernaturals differently than others. How is she handling the change?"

I snorted and turned back around to lean against him again. "About as well as can be expected. She's afraid her new revelation will scare of a potential boy who likes her." I chuckled. "Like a typical teenaged girl, she's freaked about the hard skin, claws, and deep voice."

Dad's laugh reverberated throughout my body, and I basked in its warmness. *"I can understand that. I think back to when you were that age, and I'm sure it is a difficult thing to suddenly have to deal with. But if this boy is worth his salt, he will stick."*

"That's pretty much what I told her."

I knew I needed to get up and run back home, but I didn't want to move and lose our connection.

"Hey, Dad?"

"Yes, Shayla."

"I was wondering. In my capacity as the game warden for Enchanted Island, I am in charge of the flora and fauna. And I check on most of it daily, but I haven't really taken any data on the north side of the island. I know that area is all off limits to Enchanted Island supernaturals, but I think for my job, I should keep data on the north side."

"If you feel it's wise, then I don't see any problem."

"What do you suppose there is...like thousands and thousands of uninhabited forest acres?"

"At least."

"So you don't mind me trekking around up there? You know I always want to ask before I just go there."

"*I appreciate the respect you give me and the north side of the island. And I think it's a good idea for you to monitor that area. It's vast, I know, but I've gotten word from the animals over the years that more and more supernatural citizens are pushing the boundary up there. I'd like it to remain off limits.*"

"Then I'll make sure it happens," I promised as I stood. "In a couple weeks, hopefully I'll have a lot of the northern section monitored, and I'll be able to tell you exactly what's going on up there."

"*Be careful, Daughter of my Heart, for the north part of the island can be fraught with danger.*"

****

Ready for Book 7, Deadly Client, in the Witch in the Woods series? Click here for more adventures... https://www.amazon.com/dp/B09CN3F5XW

****

Do you love the idea of a time-traveling, cold-case solving witch? Then Lexi and her side-kick detective familiar, Rex the Rat, are just what you're looking for! Check out their first stop to 1988 in Time After Time https://www.amazon.com/Time-After-Witch-Book-ebook/dp/B07MHBD6B4/ref=tmm_kin_swatch_0?_encoding=UTF8&qid=1608255390&sr=1-1-80ba0e26-a1cd-4e7b-87a0-a2ffae3a273c

Have you read the hilarious adventures of Ryli Sinclair and Aunt Shirley? Book 1 is Picture Perfect Murder! https://www.amazon.com/Picture-Perfect-Murder-Sinclair-Mystery-ebook/dp/B0182D2UL8/ref=sr_1_6?dchild=1&keywords=jenna+st.+james&qid=1587863413&sr=8-6

Love the idea of a bookstore/bar set in the picturesque wine country of Sonoma County? Then join Jaycee, Jax, Gramps, Tillie, and the whole gang as they solve murders while slinging suds and chasing bad guys in this hilarious series. https://www.amazon.com/Murder-Vine-Sullivan-Sisters-Mystery-ebook/dp/B01KECDAOQ/ref=sr_1_13?dchild=1&keywords=jenna+st.+james&qid=1594531354&sr=8-13

How about a seaside mystery? My stepdaughter and I write a mystery where high school seniors pair up with their grandma and great-aunt! Book one, Seaside & Homicide: https://www.amazon.com/Seaside-Homicide-Copper-Cove-Book-ebook/dp/B07QM1G15Z/ref=sr_1_2?dchild=1&keywords=jenna+st.+james&qid=1587863553&sr=8-2

Or maybe you're in the mood for a romantic comedy…heavy on comedy and light on sweet romance? Then the Trinity Falls series is for you! https://www.amazon.com/Blazing-Trouble-Trinity-Falls-Book-ebook/dp/B07WFX2L1C/ref=cm_cr_arp_d_product_top?ie=UTF8

Deadly Caramel

About the Author

Jenna writes in the genres of cozy/paranormal cozy/romantic comedy. Her humorous characters and stories revolve around over-the-top family members, creative murders, and there's always a positive element of the military in her stories. Jenna currently lives in Missouri with her fiancé, step-daughter, Nova Scotia duck tolling retriever dog, Brownie, and her tuxedo-cat, Whiskey. She is a former court reporter turned educator turned full-time writer. She has a Master's degree in Special Education, and an Education Specialist degree in Curriculum and Instruction. She also spent twelve years in full-time ministry.

When she's not writing, Jenna likes to attend beer and wine tastings, go antiquing, visit craft festivals, and spend time with her family and friends. Check out her website at http://www.jennastjames.com/. Don't forget to **sign up for the newsletter** so you can keep up with the latest releases! You can also friend request her on Facebook at jennastjamesauthor/ or catch her on Instagram at authorjennastjames.

Printed in Great Britain
by Amazon